At Night,
I Become a Monster

AT NIGHT, I BECOME A MONSTER

© Yoru Sumino 2016
All rights reserved.

First published in Japan in 2016 by Futabasha Publishers Ltd., Tokyo.
English version published by Seven Seas Entertainment
under license from Futabasha Publishers Ltd.

Seven Seas press and purchase enquiries can be sent to
Marketing Manager Lianne Sentar at press@gomanga.com.
Information requiring the distribution and purchase of
digital editions is available from Digital Manager CK Russell
at digital@gomanga.com.

Follow Seven Seas Entertainment online at
sevenseasentertainment.com.

TRANSLATION: Diana Taylor
ADAPTATION: Nino Cipri
COVER DESIGN: KC Fabellon
INTERIOR LAYOUT & DESIGN: Clay Gardner
PROOFREADER: Jade Gardner, Stephanie Cohen
ASSISTANT EDITOR: J.P. Sullivan
LIGHT NOVEL EDITOR: Nibedita Sen
PREPRESS TECHNICIAN: Rhiannon Rasmussen-Silverstein
PRODUCTION MANAGER: Lissa Pattillo
MANAGING EDITOR: Julie Davis
ASSOCIATE PUBLISHER: Adam Arnold
PUBLISHER: Jason DeAngelis

ISBN: 978-1-64505-297-5
Printed in Canada
First Printing: April 2020
10 9 8 7 6 5 4 3 2 1

At Night, I Become a Monster

WRITTEN BY
Yoru Sumino

TRANSLATION BY
Diana Taylor

Seven Seas

Seven Seas Entertainment

Table of Contents

At night, I become a monster.

Tuesday NIGHT

IT COMES ON SUDDENLY in the dead of night when I'm all alone in my room. It comes whether I'm sleeping or sitting or standing or squatting. It starts from my fingertips, or my navel, or sometimes my mouth.

That night, the black droplets came as tears spilling from my eyes. Mote by mote, a river of unending pitch-black tears, the streams growing gradually until they fell like two waterfalls from my eyes. The simmering, writhing black drops spread to cover my face and then flowed down my neck to my chest, arms, and waist—until every last inch of my body was covered, down to the tips of my fingers.

All colors but black drained from the surface of my body at that point. I've never had a chance to watch my body's transformation, so I have no idea what it looks like. I merely get a sense of my body *changing*. Assimilating into the black drops, into a form without skin, without flesh, without bone, a form which is no doubt dreadful to look upon. But like I said, I haven't actually *seen* it, so I couldn't actually say for certain. For all I know, maybe I look rather endearing to an outsider, like one of the soot sprites from that one movie. A *makkuro kurosuke*.

When I was finally able to see my own body, it had transformed into something like a six-legged beast made of pure darkness. As I gazed at my reflection in the full-length mirror, the only things that shone on my wavering black form were the whites of my eight eyes, set above a bottomless, inky crevice of a mouth.

The first night that I viewed my own form, the black drops on the surface of my body went wild with the shock. I nearly ended up demolishing my room. However, I found that I accepted it with unexpected ease once I tried thinking of myself as something like a monster appearing in a video game or the strange beasts that I had seen in anime. How lucky that I was born in the modern age.

When I first transformed, my body was around the size of a large dog. If I want to grow larger, I can will the black drops to move and become as large as a mountain. There was no point in enlarging myself now, though. I was still stuck in my room.

I thought then that I might go outside. Careful not to smash my window the way I did on that very first night, I sprang up lightly and squeezed myself through a tiny crack in the windowsill, slipping out of my second-story room.

My body briefly scattered like a liquid, reforming into a more aerodynamic shape as I tore through the air. In a flash, I landed soundlessly upon the ground. I was in an empty lot about three hundred meters from my home. Previously, I'd just jumped as hard and as far as I could, but after landing on a doghouse in a stranger's yard and crushing it, I decided to start aiming for more open areas. Luckily, the poor pup happened to be sleeping outside his home that time. I slipped him a bit of jerky later.

The night breeze felt good, and there was a comfortable quiet around me as I expanded my body to about three times its original size, under the gaze of a half-sleeping stray cat nearby. After testing out a variety of sizes, I had determined that this one was the most comfortable for sitting, which was the closest I could get to a comfortable resting position. Seeing this dark monster suddenly spring up beside it, the sleepy-looking stray skittered away at top speed. Sorry to have disturbed your peaceful sleep, kitty.

Now a beast as wide as a road, I strode down the empty street, my six legs moving in an insectoid rhythm. Normally, this was when I would start thinking about what I wanted to do next, but tonight I had only one destination in mind.

As I continued walking, scaring off a dog who was harassing a cat along the way, I came to a crossroads. Last night, I'd turned left here and made my way out to the sea. The shore was quiet this late, and the sound of the waves put a pleasant stop to the pulsing motion of my inky form. I still had a bit of time, so I thought perhaps I could stop by the sea again tonight before moving on to my objective.

As I let the fond memories of the night before overtake me, a scream came from off to my left. I shuddered and turned to look.

I saw a fellow who had been riding briskly along on his bicycle. He seemed to have noticed my presence just as he was about to collide with me. He let out a loud scream and toppled over on the spot. I felt badly for the poor guy, but there was nothing that I could do for him. For now, I put thoughts of the sea aside and made a break down the road in the opposite direction. Whenever I caught wind of others around, I always ran away. That guy would almost certainly think that this was all just a dream when he woke up the next morning. Of course, it wasn't a dream at all. I would still be here, the window still broken, and the doghouse still destroyed.

My quick retreat was perhaps a bit *too* speedy. Before I knew it, I ended up somewhere that I didn't recognize. Hoping to get a better grasp of where I was, I moved to a nearby park and made myself larger than a house. As I swept my gaze around, far taller than even the power poles, I found that I really had traveled an incredible distance. Far on the horizon, I could see the shore where I had spent those fleeting moments the night before.

I needed to get back home before dawn. So, for the time being, I shrunk back down until I was around the width of the road again and began leisurely making my way back towards the sea.

If I ever was discovered, the ones who found me would definitely be shocked. However, it was easy to avoid being seen. For example, if I were to see a car coming, I could just leap up high enough to pass over the car unseen. Of course, I don't really have to avoid cars. It wasn't as if I would die if one hit me, and even if it did, I could simply let them pass right through me by diffusing the black drops of my body at the point of impact. The real reason I avoided them was to prevent any accidents caused by startled drivers. Besides, I had tired of the game of frightening people long ago.

Tonight, I leapt high enough to overtake any approaching vehicles. Even with a form like this, I could feel the evening breeze. I could hear sirens wailing faintly in the distance. Night is such a peaceful time.

When I arrived at the shore, I found the lovely, familiar reflection of the moon upon the ocean.

This night, however, someone had arrived here before me. Two people sat upon the beach, their arms around each other's shoulders. I got the feeling that they had come hoping to spend a little time enjoying the ocean as well. Though they were some distance away, having a monster appear at a time like this would definitely spoil the mood. I was sad to go, but I decided to quietly leave the shore behind. I was rather proud of myself for managing to be so considerate.

Seemed I had no choice but to head straight for my objective.

From where I stood, my intended destination would take about ten minutes to reach by bike. If I were to run in this form, it would not even take ten seconds. That said, I had less and less of a reason to rush now, so I took my time heading there, so as not to startle anyone.

In the end, it took me about twenty minutes to arrive at my destination. Separated from the residences and surrounded by greenery, the place was utterly silent. I stretched my back up, literally, and peeked over the outer walls. Naturally, no one was there. Melting and dispersing my body, I slipped through a tiny hole in the wall and crept into the schoolyard.

Just a few hours prior, I had been in the bath. It was not some sort of whim that led me to return to campus, nor was I interested in causing mischief. I definitely hadn't come back because I sincerely adored the school that I attended. It was because there was a change in tomorrow's schedule, and I had left my homework in my locker.

I gathered up the black drops and reformed my monstrous body. I could see glimpses of light from inside the school building, likely a security guard making the rounds. I had to be sure not to startle him, and that meant staying out of sight.

I shrank myself down a bit, pretending to be a large dog. I hugged the edges of the schoolyard as I walked towards the building. Of course, I could pretend all I want, but if anyone got close, they would see my jagged mouth and eight eyes, my six legs and my four tails, and probably have a heart attack. Even if I could change my size, or momentarily alter my form, I seemed to be beholden to some guideline that required I maintain this basic appearance—a guideline set by whom, I don't know.

When I arrived at the closer of the two school buildings, I clung to the wall, climbing to the roof in one swift move. Hoping to make a silent entrance, I hopped clear over the chain-link fence and landed soundlessly. Honestly, I should have just slipped in through one of the windows along the way, but I hoped to take a bit of a detour.

I hadn't been up on the roof since I first toured the school as a new student. I let myself indulge in a sense of loftiness, of being above it all. The illusion was slightly marred when I happened to spot a cigarette butt on the ground nearby. For better or worse, my eyes are sharp even in the dark of night.

Once I finished relishing the feeling of the wind—and my own sense of satisfaction—I slipped in through the keyhole in the heavy door.

It was silent inside—or rather, there was a low sound, some kind of electric hum. Probably a ventilation fan or something. It wasn't pitch-black, either. The emergency lamps and the light of the moon filled the halls with a dim glow.

Still, even with the sound and the light, the school was kind of eerie at night.

If I were to bump into anyone, they would be the one most surprised. Plus, I can make myself enormous at a moment's notice if need be, so I wouldn't have any trouble even if a ghost or something popped out. All the same, I felt a chill down my back. Time to hurry up and do what I came to do and get out of here.

The school building had five floors, and the third year classroom that I was assigned to was on the third. As I slowly descended the stairs, even my black drops seemed somehow uneasy, jittering silently on the surface. I passed by the fourth floor, which held the library and the art room. The moonlight piercing through the window shone upon my dark form. There was a full moon tonight.

Though I transformed every night, I couldn't help but wonder if it would be less disruptive to my life if I only transformed into a monster during the full moon, like a werewolf or something. As I arrived at the third floor, thinking about such frivolous things, I heard the sound of running water from the bathroom right beside the staircase and immediately leapt to hide myself. Of course, it was probably just an automated cleaning system. I'm not sure what I was thinking, really, given that I never looked particularly intimidating in this form.

Step by step, I approached the classroom. Class Two—my class. As I passed by a pair of other classrooms, I felt the chambers of my heart seize. I'm not sure a heart even beat within my chest, but I felt it all the same.

The end of this infiltration—which seemed strangely long given how little time had actually passed—was now in sight. I slipped in through the crack under the door at the back of the classroom. As I entered, I felt like I had been plunged into a completely different world. It was so quiet I could feel my ears ringing.

Whoever was on cleanup duty that day was sloppy, so the rows of desks were misaligned. However, it was not my responsibility to be concerned about such things, so I quickly opened my locker with one of my tails. I hated looking inside—I intentionally messed the contents up a bit, despite my daytime self's love of order.

Inside were my math textbook, workbooks, and handouts. I kept them all in line with my tail, which I could easily control. I thought through my next steps. I would have to open up the door of the classroom and put these outside before I left, since unlike me, they were too thick to pass through the small crack beneath the door. Would exiting from the hall side be less work, or maybe the window side facing the courtyard? I definitely couldn't just drop them out from the window. Perhaps it would be better to place the bundle of materials up on the roof and then come back down later to close the window? What a bother.

I scratched my head with my tail, rather than my hands, as I always did when I was lost in thought.

Then my gaze flitted back towards the blackboard.

"What are you...do...ing?"

I had been sure I was alone.

Before me, I saw the form of a girl standing with her hands on the lectern. I was so startled by her appearance that my breath stopped. I couldn't form a single word. Instead, the sensation of goosebumps rippled across my whole body. The black drops began to writhe.

As the drops trembled, they kicked up a wind and then a storm. Papers tore from the wall. Desks went crashing to the floor. The droplets continued to rage, covering the whole classroom, even reaching out for the girl and the lectern.

"Aah!"

The cowering girl's scream finally quelled the storm within my heart. The droplets ceased their rampage, and though they still seemed a bit distraught, they slowly started to return to my body. Despite their return, they refused to settle into their typical state. My whole body swelled, pulsing with violent, quivering waves.

The girl stared at me, as though she had only just barely worked up the courage to speak. I met her eyes with two of my eight. *Why? Just how on Earth? Here? At a time like this?*

I'm sure that she had a lot of questions about me, but I had just as many about her.

We stared at each other in silence.

I still hadn't forgotten that I meant to escape—I was merely concerned. I didn't know whether she had seen me fiddling with the lockers, nor if she had spotted the textbook lying at my feet, nor what I ought to do if she had.

She had me completely off balance.

"Y-y-y-y-y-you scared…me."

She suddenly began to tremble, as though in delayed shock. Or perhaps she was a little slow on the uptake and had previously set her shock aside.

The girl looked around suspiciously, eyes roving the room, shoulders swaying from side to side. She appeared to be trying to determine just what position she'd been put into. I watched her, unsure of what to do. I don't know whether she came to some silent conclusion, but she turned towards me and held out both hands, palms out flat.

"W-wait… Wait a…mi…mi…minute…"

She hurried out of the classroom. Apparently, the front door was already unlocked.

I took a brief look behind me and resolved to put the girl's reason for being here and the meaning of her actions aside. I frantically gathered up my textbook bundle and shut my locker.

Once I had hidden the evidence of my identity, a number of thoughts began to run through my head. Why was she here at a time like this, and where had she gone? And moreover, how was it that she could even bring herself to speak to a monster?

Honestly, I should have just run away while my head was still racked with confusion, leaving those questions unanswered. But I began to worry about whether she'd been caught by the school nightguard.

And so I waited.

Relatively soon after, she returned, a satisfied grin upon her face.

"I'm baaack. I went and...explained everything, so...it's fine... now."

Explained? I began to ask but abruptly stopped myself. I had no idea how my voice sounded to other people. If it was the same as normal, she might end up realizing who I was. I needed to avoid that possibility.

With that thought in mind, I should have dodged the question, but I began to wonder. How *did* my voice sound when I was a monster? Both she and I were soon to learn the answer to that question.

"So...any...way, what were you...doing?"

I did not reply.

"You're...Acchi-kun, aren't you?"

"Huh?"

A strange voice came out of my unsuccessfully stopped-up mouth. There it was.

A cold sweat—or so it felt; who knows whether or not sweat was actually there—ran along my whole body. The pulsing waves that I had been trying to suppress grew again in magnitude.

How'd she know it was me?

I glanced behind me. She had seen my locker after all, hadn't she?

"Oh, your voice...does...sound like Acchi-kun's."

She clapped her hands together very deliberately. The fact that it was the middle of the night, and that she was standing in front of a monster, didn't stop her nearly irritating theatrics.

I did not reply. Instead, I tried raising a bit of a growl, thinking that I might be able to force her conclusion back out of her head. I knew that I could howl, at least. I'd done it before to chase away a stray dog.

She tilted her head, and I thought for a moment that she might be having second thoughts about me.

"Are you...hun...gry?"

Nope. Still speaking in that strange rhythm, punctuated in a peculiar way that made it difficult to follow, she approached me until she stood just before my eyes, her feet tapping across the floor. She peered into my face. I tried to back away, forgetting my own immense size, but I was trapped.

What could I do? I should have run away at once. However, if I were to leave now, and she tried to tell others that she'd met me as a monster in the middle of the night... Well, even if no one believed her, it would eliminate the distance that I had previously kept between us. That was no good.

She could probably tell that I was shaken. A vapid smile of self-satisfaction spread across her face.

"Aaah...well."

I maintained silence.

"If you try...to pretend you aren't...Acchi-kun...then I...might have to start...spreading rumors."

"Wai—! Ah, no, uh—!"

I inadvertently let my voice return to normal as I bristled at her threat. Her smile widened, as though perhaps she was pleased to have heard my voice.

"It's...fiiine."

What was fine?

"I won't...t-tell...anyone!"

I had no idea what was supposed to be reassuring about those wholly untrustworthy words.

"And in re...turn, you can't...tell anyone that I was...here. O...kie dokie?"

I was a little startled at her proposition.

Bargaining terms. I'd thought she was some kind of idiot, someone who couldn't read the situation. Apparently, I was wrong.

She stared at me with her great big eyes.

I had lost.

After thinking on it, I nodded. I figured it was better to agree to a bargain where both sides could blackmail the other, rather than leave myself open to uncertainty, not knowing what might happen next. It was far too dangerous to let her run loose—this girl who knew the me behind the monster. She was the kind of person who always said more than she needed to.

Thinking about it afterwards, perhaps I *wanted* someone to know that I could turn into a monster. Some part of me probably wanted to take pride in it.

I steeled myself, taking care that my voice would not betray me. "All right," I said—and as I did, the girl once again gave that smile.

"Won...der...ful," she replied.

I wasn't sure I agreed. What would have been most wonderful was not getting caught by that girl at all.

...Right. Speaking of. What *was* this girl doing sneaking into school in the middle of the night? As I worried over whether or not to interrogate her, she spoke first. A peculiar question crossed her lips.

"Acchi-kun, is that...a...kigurumi?"

I swiftly dodged as she reached her arms out, trying to touch my front legs. I was unsure what might happen if a person touched me. Would anyone else really dare to touch me so suddenly? Who could imagine this form of mine to be a *costume?*

"It's not."

"Ah... I see. So...it isn't. It doesn't seem like you're...wearing a kigurumi...right now."

Though I tried to speak with a threatening edge to my voice, this girl was not one to be so easily intimidated. Once again, she tried to touch me. What was with her? She was such a...

Actually, what was with all the "Acchi-kun, Acchi-kun?"

"I don't recall you ever calling me 'Acchi' before."

In attempting to speak normally, caught up in the flow of the conversation, I inadvertently outed myself as "Acchi" out loud. However, this girl was already someone who spoke to a monster as though it were her normal classmate. She deliberately shook her head, like such small details did not concern her.

"I have...not. But that's what...you're called, isn't it? I am...Yano Satsuki, don't...you remember? Do you like to...use nicknames? Or...normal names?"

"...Full names. Yano-san, what are you doing here? In this classroom?"

"I came...to play. But this is...out of hand. Let's...fix this."

Without awaiting my reply, Yano-san began to right the desks that I had knocked over. I couldn't just stand there and watch her fix the mess that I had made, so I began to straighten the desks one by one with my tail. "How...convenient," she said, softly.

After rearranging the desks more neatly than they had been when I arrived and fixing the timetables back to the wall, she looked at me and then made a gesture as though wiping sweat from her brow.

"Thanks...for the help."

"No big."

We had never once been together in any group or student council or club. I felt no comfortable sense of accomplishment from working with this girl. I'd never even desired to speak to her before now.

Yano-san pounded her fist once. "That's...right."

I wasn't sure what she was going to say, but I got the sense that something strange was going to come out of her mouth again. However, it was an unexpectedly straightforward question.

"You were ques...tioning me...but before that...I'm so curious to know, if that's... not a kigu...rumi, then how is it you look...like that, Acchi...kun?"

I had no idea what to tell her, but I thought that I better at least say something and opened my mouth to speak. Just then, suddenly, a familiar sound rang throughout the classroom.

I must be sensitive to sounds, because I recoiled in shock.

I had no idea that the school bells chimed even at night. Though there were a few homes around the campus. You'd think that it would be considered a disturbance of the peace.

When I looked at Yano-san, however, she did not appear surprised at all. This must not have been the first time that she snuck into the school if she knew that the bells would chime. However, things were a little more complicated than that.

"Ah... Looks like...midnight break is...coming to an...end."

She pulled her phone from her pocket and fiddled with it, and the chiming stopped.

"Wh-what was that noise?"

"That was...the warning bell. If I...don't hear the...chime, I'll... forget. Midnight...break will be over in ten...minutes."

What on earth was "midnight break?" Just as I began to fume over Yano-san talking nonsense on top of her strange actions, she held both of her palms out towards me. Perhaps she couldn't tell how disgruntled I was underneath my dark, monstrous face.

"Let's...continue this...tomorrow."

"T-tomorrow?"

Did she mean during school? No way. Absolutely, positively not. There was no way I would be seen speaking to Yano-san, let alone risk looking chummy with her.

"Um, Yano-san..."

"It's...fiiine! I don't mean during...the day. Try and come here...a little earlier...tomorrow night."

"Here?"

"Yes...here. Can you...come?"

Though Yano-san didn't say it, the threat was implied that if I did not come, she would start telling everyone. The effect of her holding that fact over me was immediate. Though we ostensibly had a mutual agreement, if that agreement was broken, the damage would fall disproportionately on my side.

Having no other choice, I nodded.

What an utter, tremendous turn this night had taken, that despite this monstrous form of mine, I should be ordered around by such a weird girl.

Annoyed at the look of joy on Yano-san's face, I slipped through a tiny crack in the window and leapt outside without another word.

It wasn't until the sun was rising and my human form returned that I realized I had forgotten my homework.

My entire evening had been an utter waste.

At Night,
I Become a Monster

Wednesday
DAY

SINCE I STARTED becoming a monster, I no longer sleep at night.

However, for the first time in ages, I thought that it all might have just been a dream. There was absolutely no rational explanation behind my becoming a monster and going to school in the middle of the night, only to find a girl from class there and have a conversation with her—let alone agreeing to a secret meeting. For all I knew, maybe the past weeks of my becoming a monster were all just a vivid dream, too.

Though reckless and unfortunate, no matter how you slice it, that kind of thinking is normal. Honestly, even if it *was* a dream, there still had to be something wrong with me. That was some imagination. Transforming into a monster and meeting *Yano* of all people?

I hopped on my bike and set off for school, clinging to my comfortable delusion right up until I spotted the ruined doghouse. There aren't words to describe the way looking at it made me feel.

"Yo, Acchi!"

Someone punched me lightly in the back as I stood at my shoe box. I already knew who it was, but I made a show of surprise as I turned around.

"Morning. Oh, did you change your hair?"

"Heh heh, somehow, having another man notice it doesn't really do it for me!" Kasai had a toothy grin on his face as he took a dancing step into his indoor shoes. Kasai was a great deal shorter than me, so I was quick to notice his new flair. Standing at the foot of the stairs, I was wondering whether someone might find fault with it when a voice came from behind us.

"Kasai, you get rid of that perm immediately."

My petrified friend and I both turned to see the school nurse standing there, grimacing. Her name was Noto.

"You don't expect me to shave it off, do you?" Somehow Kasai always managed to crack a joke in the face of a warning, no matter who the teacher was.

"There's no point in a punishment if it doesn't make you reflect on your actions," she said and walked away.

What might she say to me if she knew that I had snuck into the school? I began to wonder, letting my mind run wild with all kinds of terrible scenarios, as Kasai once again moved to climb the steps. I followed quickly behind.

"Acchi, were you starin' at Non-chan there? You got a thing for old ladies?"

"No way. And anyway, she's not *that* old."

"Isn't she like thirty?"

The hallway was packed when we reached the third floor. Our teachers kept telling us that this would be the year we needed to focus on our exams, but the reality of that had yet to really sink in for us. I turned towards the classroom and took one step, and then another. Naturally, my gaze was drawn to my classroom. My classmates swarmed in and out of the entrance of that box, like ants from a mound.

One of them walked towards us, so Kasai raised his hand and gave them a mild greeting. Then someone else came out from the other side and caught my gaze. A shiver ran down my spine. The girl, just now leaving the classroom, waved the cleaning cloth she held in one hand. She began walking our way with a satisfied grin.

Yano Satsuki found us, as smug as you please. She opened her mouth to chat as though everything were completely normal. "Good mor...*ning.*"

She greeted us in her weird way, the emphases and pauses in her words all wrong. The two of us said nothing until we passed her by, not even looking in the direction of her voice. I patted my chest in relief.

There was such a ruckus in the classroom that you could hear it from the hallway. We entered the room, Kasai greeted everyone, and the whole class reacted. I managed a greeting of my own, but that got lost in the mirth surrounding Kasai. Thank goodness he decided to change his hair that day. While everyone was busy ribbing him, I slipped into my seat, blending into the background. My face pretty much said, *What? I've been here the whole time.*

I moved my math textbook from my locker to my desk. It was the same book I'd bungled bringing home last night. I should have used the time I had left to complete my homework, but I couldn't think of anyone in my class who would have tried to make that kind of desperate recovery. Not because of one piddly little homework assignment, anyway. I couldn't bear the thought of being laughed at as some kind of study freak, so I had no choice but to keep my head down for the day and admit to forgetting.

With that decision made, I had nothing in particular to occupy myself with during that morning period, so I just passed the time fiddling pointlessly with my phone, exchanging greetings and making light conversation with the students in the surrounding seats as they arrived. Really, it wasn't so bad. Kudou sat down at the seat next to mine, her double teeth poking out from a toothy smile. She'd been in the same class as me since we were first years, so we always got on well.

After some time, Yano returned, her cleaning cloth swaying in her hands. Water from the cloth dripped onto the floor, like she hadn't wrung it out properly. I can't say that made her any more popular with the people around her. As I wondered what she intended to do with such an excessively wet cloth, she moved over to her own desk and began leisurely wiping down the top. I caught the spectacle out of the corner of my eye. From my seat in the very back, Yano's was situated two squares away diagonally, a quick hop for a bishop in chess or shogi. I wasn't exactly sure what was up with Yano's desk that it needed cleaning, but it was obvious that *something* had happened.

Once she was satisfied with her careful cleaning job (or maybe she had simply given up), Yano walked toward the front of the classroom again, swinging her cloth in her hand. Just as she passed by Kasai and the others, who were still loitering in the front, she called out in a lilting voice. "You changed...your hair!" Something about her manner was just...*inconsiderate,* somehow. That same self-satisfied smile sat upon her face. Naturally, not a single one of them looked her way. Yano didn't fail to notice. She was used to it. She had barely any reaction to the lack of reaction as she exited the classroom.

Once she left, a number of kids clicked their tongues loudly. It was business as usual for Yano. If I started worrying about her, I would never stop.

Either way, I had nothing to do at the moment, so I decided to head for the bathroom. I stepped out into the hall and started walking in the opposite direction of where Yano had headed. The set of bathrooms where she was probably off dampening her cloth again was definitely closer, but if we ran into each other and she tried to talk to me, it would be a pain. She probably wouldn't say anything about the night before, not wanting to be found out herself, but even so.

After carefully washing my hands for I'm not sure how long, I stepped back out into the hall to see Midorikawa Futaba standing nearby.

What a name. It felt like the kind of name only an actress or a manga character could have. She held a book in one hand and glanced my way, a sour look on her face. Her long hair fell to her back, swaying. It gave me a bit of whiplash to deal with two girls with such drastically contrasting personalities first thing in the morning. However, I wasn't about to let that feeling overwhelm me. I put on a little smile, the same kind of smile I might give to anybody.

"Morning," I said.

"Mm," Midorikawa signaled back in a tiny voice. The corners of her mouth raised so subtly that I couldn't tell whether or not she was smiling. Without saying another word, she turned towards the classroom and walked off, as though she had no recollection of ever having met me. It wasn't that she was mad, though. That was just how she always was.

I followed behind her, this girl who was the polar opposite of Yano. They couldn't be more different. Yano was always grinning and saying unnecessary things in that loud voice of hers.

As Midorikawa entered the classroom, a few students standing near the entrance brightly greeted her. "Good morning!"

She replied to them collectively with another "Mm," and a nod, heading to her seat without so much as a word of greeting.

As she sat down, a girl at a nearby seat piped up. "Futaba-chan, were you at the library again?"

Midorikawa replied to the question with yet another "Mm" and opened up her book. Clearly, she had no interest in making conversation. Unbothered, the other girl simply turned to another classmate and began chatting with them instead, not seeming at all displeased.

Midorikawa, though as thick as Yano when it came to reading the room, received completely different treatment than the class's whipping girl. There were all kinds of reasons why.

As I passed the time in meandering conversation with my seat neighbor, Kudou, I once again caught a glimpse of Yano in the corner of my eye. She was sitting in her seat, with no one else around, swinging her legs with a smile on her face.

Finally, the bell rang. Our homeroom teacher, Koike, arrived. As long as the flow of our homeroom and lessons proceeded in their usual way, everything would be fine. I could relax.

I completely ignored our first period of language arts, and when I spoke up during math lessons in second period, the teacher merely said, "That's unusual."

It wasn't at all, though. I often forgot my homework, though I usually didn't stand up and admit as much. I was directed to be sure to bring it in tomorrow and then returned to my own desk.

After third period's geography class came to a close, we approached the least relaxing class of all: P.E.

As we walked to the locker rooms, the girls held a large-scale rock-paper-scissors tourney right in front of Yano, to see who she would be foisted off on. Ah, of course. There were an even number of girls present today. Did the gym teacher really think that it was a coincidence that Yano always ended up the odd kid out when forming warm-up pairs? Did the adults really not remember their own time in junior high?

We were all far crueler creatures than any of the adults imagined.

As we changed, moved to the gym, and started playing something like dodgeball, the teacher blew the whistle. Once warm-ups were through, we remained in pairs and practiced volleyball serves, while the students in the athletics clubs watched us and offered assistance. One had to be at least decent at it to not stand out.

We split the gym in two between boys and girls and continued our lessons. After giving Kasai a high-five, I happened to look towards the girls. Midorikawa had pulled back her long hair, something she did only for gym. She'd just suffered defeat from a ball served by Iguchi. Just beyond her, I saw Yano lying on the floor, face-up towards the ceiling. Something white was fluttering from her nostrils, so she must have gotten a nosebleed. Some of the girls were observing her, but no one approached.

"Acchi, who are you lookin' at? Do you need little Kasai-chan here to help you out?" said Kasai, grinning.

I replied with a casual "Shut up," and returned to the court.

Kasai returned to the court after me, lagging behind when the teacher reprimanded him. He had surely been looking at someone as well. Well, not *someone*. It was more specific than that, which was probably why he had assumed that I was doing the same.

"Nice work, every...one," Yano said to us in the same way that she spoke to the other girls.

Sure enough, as class ended, the tissues sprouting from Yano's stopped-up nose were dyed with blood. When nobody replied to her, Yano began trudging towards me, her small body swaying. I turned around and prayed with all my might that she would not bring up anything from the night before. It was Yano, after all, so I couldn't rule out the possibility.

But I didn't need to worry. Yano did no such thing. That said, she *was* always causing trouble for the people around her, whether by her inability to read a room or because she simply was unaware of her surroundings.

I was talking to everyone else, trying my hardest not to lay eyes upon Yano's small receding form, when suddenly, she crouched down—or so it seemed. I wasn't...actually looking at where I was going. And so, I didn't notice until it was almost too late, and though I panicked and tried at the last moment to avoid her, I inadvertently ended up kicking her right leg. When I unthinkingly turned back to look, she was on the ground on her backside, the bloody tissues on the floor in front of her.

Yano looked up at me, seemingly with great shock. I said nothing.

Still saying nothing, as if nothing had happened at all, I returned to my conversation with Kasai and the others. The others did not question this.

From behind, I heard a voice say, "You sur...prised me..." but I did not turn around.

Eventually, I followed the others in the crowd flowing back into the boys' locker room and was getting changed when a heavy hand struck me in the shoulder. It was Motoda of the baseball club. He wasn't even scowling at me or anything. He was actually grinning.

"You totally kicked her, didn't you?" He spoke in a loud voice, so loud that those out in the hallway probably overheard.

I just shrugged as I shed my gym clothes and replied, "She shouldn't have crouched down all of a sudden in front of me." Motoda whistled.

As I finished changing my clothes, I was suddenly struck with a gnawing hunger. Ever since I first became a monster, I would grow ravenous completely at random. Up next was lunch. Our school didn't serve set meals, so when the bell rang, there was a small stampede towards the cafeteria. I followed that stampede, purchased a meal ticket, and snagged myself some udon and katsudon.

As I sat down diagonally across from Kasai, who had already begun eating his ramen, he grinned, teeth bared. "You're gonna get fat, Acchi!" He cackled, good-natured.

After taking a healthy bite of my cutlet, I replied, "*Hut upff.*"

It was that natural, unguarded smile of his that made Kasai so popular with both girls and boys. After a large contingent of our cafeteria-going classmates had gathered at our table, Kasai suddenly piped up. "Oh yeah, Acchi, have you heard?"

"Heard what?"

"I heard there's been sightings of a kaiju at night, lately."

Unthinkingly, I dropped the meat that I'd been holding between my chopsticks into the udon.

"Huh? A kaiju?"

Perhaps at how clumsily I had shown my surprise, the whole table burst into laughter.

"Yeah, there've been a bunch of people lately saying that they saw it! Like, they looked out in the middle of the night and there was this huuuge thing. They thought at first that it was just a dream, but they've all been sayin' the same thing—that it's got a bunch of eyes, and a bunch of legs, and it's all creepy-crawly."

"Would be pretty scary to see something super big like that," I replied, making what I hoped was a skeptical face. I carried the dashi-soaked cutlet into my mouth, which should have been delicious, but I was so focused on Kasai that I couldn't taste it at all.

"So, wanna go look for it?"

"It comes out in the middle of the night, doesn't it? I'll be asleep."

"Whaaat? Acchi, you're so serious!"

I suppose to Kasai, who had been caught sneaking out of his house in the middle of the night in order to meet his girlfriend, refusing an invitation on the grounds of an early bedtime seemed an awfully straight-laced thing to do. It was only after I thought that I better try to avoid bumping into Kasai during his nighttime excursions that it occurred to me: Even if I was seen, no one would ever know that it was me...short of seeing me digging through my locker, anyway.

Nevertheless, the rumor of the monster's existence appeared to be spreading.

"Kasai, stop it! Acchi isn't like you!"

With that, a burst of laughter rang out. One of the girls added, "That's right, you stay away from Acchi!" to yet another laugh. Acchi, Acchi, they called, but everyone was looking at Kasai. I was looking his way as well, laughing along.

"Enough, enough! Whatever, I'm done eating. Let's go play soccer!" Kasai stood up to ward off everyone's teasing, for some reason scratching his head and looking at me. After I unthinkingly nodded, he turned an appraising eye to one of the other boys and set about confirming we had the numbers for a game. As always, the girls looked at the boys hurriedly stuffing the rest of their meals into their mouths and laughed. "Don't you get bored of doing that every day?"

We spent the remaining thirty minutes of midday break on soccer, powering through despite our full bellies. Honestly, I wasn't very good at it, but all I had to do was run around the others to assist, so I didn't think too hard about it. We each have our own roles and positions in life. That's something we all need to understand about one another.

Not that it was something that *she* understood.

My attention had drifted away from the soccer game, dwelling on what was to come that night. I was growing a bit depressed and didn't notice when the ball came flying my way. I collided with a burly member of the basketball club. I was unprepared and already off-balance—I fell flat onto my butt.

"What happened?! Acchi! Ah! Your elbow, it's bleeding!"

Kasai alone came running over to me, the game continuing on without us. When I looked at my elbow, sure enough, I'd gotten a scrape.

"Should I take you to the nurse's office?" he asked me, his lively voice ringing out as the soccer ball flew into one of the goals.

"I'm not a kid, I'm fine," I said. "But I'll probably head over there and get it disinfected."

Kasai stared at me for a moment and then grinned. "I see." He continued, "I seeee, Acchi. You let yourself get hurt on purpose just so you could go see Non-chan! That's why you don't want me to come!"

"No way," I said, returning his smile.

Kasai replied, "That's what you mean about not being a kid, huh?" Then he ran back towards the others, who were all standing still by the goal.

Kasai would probably make some excuse for me later. As I returned from the field to the school building, I felt at ease.

Just as I'd said, I decided to head to the nurse's office and have Noto disinfect my wound. When I knocked on the door, her reply came immediately. The smell when I opened the door was a delightful one. It wasn't the smell of disinfectants; it was a calming smell. I got the same kind of feeling you get when you reach home base during a game of tag.

There were no other students in her office, so Noto appeared to be reading a library book atop her desk: *No Longer Human*. I'd never read it, but I did have to wonder if it was about turning into a monster at night or something like that.

"'Scuse me, I got a scrape. I was wondering if you could disinfect it."

"Of course. Haven't seen you in a while, Adachi-kun."

Except when she was angry, Noto always addressed students with "-kun" and "-san."

"You saw me this morning."

"I mean in here."

I sat down on the stool, and Noto quickly tended to my wound. It was only a scrape, so she didn't bandage it.

I gave her my thanks and moved to leave, when she called out, "Wait." When I looked at her, she asked, "How have you been lately?"

"How...? I mean, I've been pretty okay."

Obviously I couldn't tell her that I'd begun turning into a monster in the middle of the night. If I did, I'm sure she would have sent me straight into counseling.

"There's still thirty minutes left of break, so why don't you have a rest? You shouldn't push yourself."

"...Nah, my friends are waiting."

With a word of parting, I excused myself. My heart was beating a little faster than usual.

Noto could be harsh when issuing reprimands, but she was conscientious as a school nurse. While it was true that there were many students who found her bothersome, I wasn't one of them. So it wasn't out of any sort of malice that I chose to ignore her advice.

It was because I worried that somehow, perhaps Noto was just like Yano. Somehow, she might discern my true form.

Logically, there was no way that could be the case. Even so, thanks to what had happened the night before, I was struck by paranoia.

Now that I thought about it, I began to grow angry with Yano.

Of course, perhaps I'd only gotten what I deserved. I usually left school with Kasai, and the other day, the two of us had been loitering around the classroom. Because we left school a bit later than everyone else, I'd noticed that Motoda of the baseball club and his friends seemed to be amusing themselves doing something to Yano's shoe box. I'd kept quiet about it.

So maybe this was a bit of justice, after all.

At Night,
I Become a Monster

Wednesday
NIGHT

THAT NIGHT, after I transformed, I headed to the school with a heavy heart.

I entered the classroom via the same route as the night before, but Yano-san wasn't there. I started to grow fairly irritated at her absence. She'd told me to come early, hadn't she? I tried to tell myself that perhaps she might be hiding—but no, she really wasn't there. Was she running late? Or was she not going to come at all? The latter would be just fine, I thought, adjusting myself to a comfortable sitting size and planting myself in the back of the classroom, when suddenly the front door flung forcefully open.

"You're here...already."

"You told me to come, didn't you?" I complained, but Yano-san appeared to pay me no mind.

"Oh... I'll go wash...my hands," she said and once again exited the classroom. What was with this girl?

Shortly, she returned, rubbing her hands on her skirt to dry them. Now that I thought about it, why *was* she still in her uniform? I hadn't bothered to consider it the night before.

"I was...just dig...ging...a grave."

I hadn't asked her, but Yano-san explained why she'd been absent all the same.

"A grave?"

"Yes, a frog...got stuck in...my shoe box and died...there. Poor thing." Without prompting, she continued, "It was such...a little thing."

She held her thumb and index finger a short distance apart, indicating its size.

"Do...you pre...fer tree frogs...or horned frogs?"

"...I like Keroppi."

"Oh, I see."

Her dispassionate attitude really rubbed me the wrong way. Yano-san dutifully took her own seat and then looked my way, her legs dangling.

"Eight...eyes. Six...legs. A lot of...tails."

I began to feel like an anatomical model as she pointed out the features of my body one by one. I couldn't tell you why exactly, but the whole thing made me feel kind of weird.

I thought that she might ask me why I assumed this form, so I had prepared my answer ahead of time: "I don't know." It was a perfectly honest answer. However, the question she *did* ask caught me completely off guard.

"Is that...your real form?"

"...Huh?"

"Why...do you...change into a...human?"

I had never even considered the possibility. She was totally off-base. I told her truthfully, "I transform when night falls." I suddenly felt embarrassed, realizing how much the word *transform* made it sound like I thought I was some kind of superhero.

"I thought...for sure that you had...been born in *that*...form."

"If that were true, I wouldn't bother turning into a human and going to school."

"I thought that...you might...change into a human because it's...difficult to...live in a strange form like...that."

It hurt to be called "strange." Even imagining it vividly, it didn't seem like a very difficult life. At the very least, no worse than Yano-san's every day.

"Yano-san, why do *you* come to school?"

Behind my question was the unspoken barb: *It doesn't seem like a fun place for you to be at all.* I had meant it in a retaliatory way, but her reply was indifferent.

"I don't...have a break during...the day, so I...like to play during...midnight break."

I had no idea what she meant. I seemed to recall her saying something about "midnight break" the night before as well.

"So what is 'midnight break,' anyway?"

"You want to...hear?"

"...I mean, not really."

"Midnight break is... Well... Oh... That's it... How do you think I...get in here?"

"Dunno."

"You want to...know?"

She was such a pain in the butt. I already knew as much, of course, but talking to her one-on-one just reaffirmed the point. As I waited in frustrated silence, she began to answer a question that no one had asked.

"The security guard looks...the other...way. Only for one... hour every night. *That* is...midnight break."

"That's ridiculous."

If that was true, it was information that thieves would be dying to know.

"It's not a...lie. Obviously, it's...only for students."

And just what was obvious about that? That *obviously* wouldn't be acceptable for students, either. Not that I, standing there, was in any position to talk.

"I knew the...one be...fore...too. There...were, um...three guards whose...names I heard but forgot, but...they were all...nice peo...ple."

For them to have been "nice people" meant that not only had Yano-san met with the guards and talked to them, but those guards had neglected their duties and allowed her to remain here. If that story was true, I couldn't imagine what would have persuaded them. The more I thought about it, the more obvious it seemed that such a thing could never have happened.

"You don't...believe me...huh?" she asked.

"Believe that you come here because of some kind of midnight break?"

"Well, you were...here too yest...erday, Acchi...kun."

"I came here to collect my math book. We had homework from it."

"You're so...serious."

I doubt that Yano-san had intended to tease me, but hearing what my friends had said to me at lunchtime again now, not knowing whether it *was* her intention, I felt a pained flutter in my gut.

"I come...here to en...joy midnight...break." It wasn't the proper timing for it at all, but Yano-san grinned. "Since I...don't get to...rest dur...ing the day at...school."

How could she possibly be smiling about that? I wondered. When I didn't say something like "I see," or, "That's not true," she withdrew her smile and asked something strange.

"Acchi...kun, do...you have a...midday break?"

I didn't answer either way. I simply stayed quiet. And then, I thought about my break that day. I had shoveled down a katsudon, played soccer, gotten hurt, and met with Noto-sensei. Now that I thought about it, I wasn't actually sure that I *had* gotten a break.

"Well...then. Let's leave the talk of...daytime there."

Even though she was the one that started it.

"We still have...some time in mid...night break. What...shall we...do?"

"Uh, well, I was just thinking of going home."

"How do...you normally pass the time...at night, Acchi...kun?"

"What do I do at night?"

"I don't mean...that in a dirty...way."

Seeing this idiot say such a weird thing with such a straight face, I let out a big sigh. I couldn't help myself, hearing Yano-san say something so typical of a normal junior high-schooler.

"At night, I usually go to the beach, or the mountains," I told her.

"So, you go...wherever you want... That's nice."

"I used to go around scaring people who were out walking, but I got tired of that."

"Must be...hard to be a...ghost."

"After that—oh, right—I tried going to a theme park. I was surprised that there were a lot of employees still working there after hours."

"Really?! They...must have thought...you were some...kind of new at...traction, Acchi-kun."

Yano-san listened to my tales, giving exaggerated reactions in between. I was a bit surprised; I'd never expected such interest from her. "What about you, Yano-san? What do you do at school?"

"I watch vi...deos on my phone and...read manga, even though those are...both against school...rules."

The rules weren't in effect right now. If they were, we would probably have been breaking a lot more than just those two.

"Why not just do it at home?"

"That's not...the point."

She looked at me straight on. Unthinkingly, I averted all eight of my eyes. I didn't understand, but if Yano-san said that wasn't the point, then I guess it wasn't. It wasn't that I understood her, but that she clearly had her own code. Of course, everyone has their own code, but hers was probably more extreme. A product of her current circumstances. Thus, it was probably pointless to try and understand.

"But come...to think of it, there is some...thing to what you...said, Acchi...kun."

While it was surprising that anything I'd said to her had actually sunk in, I was grateful. At any rate, it looked like my quiet evenings might return to me.

"Let's ex...plore the...school," she said.

"...Yeah, no thanks."

"But you were...saying I should...do some...thing that I can't...do at...home."

"No, I wasn't. I was saying we should *go* home."

"I will...go home. In another thirty min...utes."

She took out her phone and checked the time. Somehow, it seemed peculiar to see her holding a phone. Did she ever actually contact anyone with that thing?

"Let's go...then."

Without even waiting for my answer, she stood up and moved to exit out the front door of the classroom. I thought for a moment—and while I was endlessly unenthused about this—I resigned myself to shrinking down to the size of a large dog and following her for now. I worried that if she was caught by the guard, she might tell him about me.

And truthfully, I can't say that I wasn't a little bit interested in what the school building was like at night.

After Yano-san left the classroom, I closed and locked the door, then slipped out into the hallway in the form of droplets.

When I shifted back into monster form, the girl gave a small round of applause.

"You really...didn't have...to close it," she said.

Now that I considered it, if this whole midnight break thing was fake, then how *did* she unlock the door?

"At that...size, you're kind...of like a...pet."

"We should be careful."

As I lowered my voice, she clapped her hands over her own mouth and said, "We're playing phan...tom thief."

It took me a few seconds to reassemble her words back into "phantom thief" in my head.

After several more steps down the hall, she pointed at my face and asked, "Can you...stretch out your...eyes?" She pointed right at them, in case there was any doubt which eyes she meant.

"Nope. Or at least I don't think I can."

"It'd...be pretty con...venient if...you could stretch...them out really far and look...around cor...ners, huh?"

While it *would* be useful for reconnaissance, other than that, the uses of such a skill would be limited. Plus, it was difficult to even picture.

Even if it wasn't a trick I could manage, the more I thought about it, the cooler it sounded.

Maybe I could transfer just a little bit of the black droplets from my body into the shadows cast by the moonlight peeking in through the windows, to create a second monster, a Shadow. It would function just like a support character from a video game, and operate by my will, making reconnaissance within the school a breeze. Having an ability like that would be so cool.

"Acchi...kun," Yano-san called out to me, walking alongside. I looked at her, but she didn't look back. Instead, she was gazing slightly behind me.

"Can you...do some...thing like...that?"

I looked back to where she indicated and was immediately startled.

"Maybe, you know...a clone...technique?"

I could only shake my head. I had no idea of what *that* was.

Behind me loomed the very thing I'd imagined: a second monster. Pure black, it followed us step for step. It differed from me in one important way—the portion where the eyes should be was all black. I was certain that there had been nothing there moments ago. When I looked out the window, the moon was shining in from roughly ahead of me.

Temporarily ignoring Yano-san, who was staring curiously at the Shadow, I tried commanding it.

Move.

I pictured it running forward, flying past me. I was skeptical, but it couldn't hurt to try.

After a few seconds' lag, the Shadow moved, roughly as I had imagined. Careful not to break my concentration, I had it continue down the hallway and around the next corner.

It surprised me to see the Shadow behaving exactly as I ordered it to. I guess I really did have that ability after all.

Just as I thought that simply making the thing move wasn't particularly good for reconnaissance, a second viewpoint suddenly appeared inside of my head. It seemed I was seeing from the Shadow's point of view, beyond the corner.

What a useful body this was.

"It's...gone."

"It's our lookout. Let's continue."

"How profes...sional."

She must have been talking about our phantom thief game again.

"Yano-san, where is it you wanted to go?"

"Maybe the mu...sic room. I want...to see if it's true what... they say a...bout pi...anos playing at...night."

"Was there some kind of urban legend about that?"

"Well...there often...are, anyway."

"That's vague."

Yano-san gave another self-satisfied smile at my retort. Just what was so funny?

Thanks to the Shadow's reconnaissance, I confirmed that there appeared to be no one between our current location and the music room above. Just in case, I checked the hall to the left and right but saw no one there, either. I didn't want to look at Yano-san's hunched back, so I walked a bit ahead. Following right behind her made me look a bit too much like a pet for my tastes.

We climbed the stairs and finally arrived at the music room at the end of the fifth floor. I entered first and unlocked the door— the opposite of the way we'd left the classroom before. Within the music room, which was encased in soundproofed padding, the grand piano was as eerie as a monster itself. It lingered there, shrouded in tense silence. It seemed like the sort of thing that very well might eat somebody alive.

"The pia...no isn't...playing."

Obviously not. No spirit would bother lingering in the mortal world just to surprise someone who came barging in like this.

The Shadow stayed outside as our lookout. If anyone were to come, they would surely run away in shock.

As I stood around aimlessly, suddenly I was startled by a twanging sound. A single wave ran through the black droplets. When I turned to look, Yano-san had opened the lid of the grand piano and taken a seat on the bench. She was so short that when she sat, she looked very much like an elementary schooler at a recital.

"Acchi...kun, are you a Moz...art fan? Or a Vi...valdi fan?"

"I prefer Beethoven," I replied. "Also, the sound of that piano really can't be good."

"Beetho...ven, huh?"

Not heeding my warning, she began to strike the keys with her tiny hands—four times in sequence. A dissonant chord reverberated throughout the room. I immediately withdrew my body and slipped into a box of cleaning supplies. Pretty quickly, I realized that if I was found, I could just scare the person away. Yano-san was the one who might end up having a hard time.

I slipped back out.

I had the Shadow check the perimeter outside the room. Apparently, the sound-proofing in this room was the real deal, as even after some time passed, no one appeared to be coming.

Yano-san looked my way, not appearing particularly panicked. "Is this...what fate feels...like?"

"You think that was *fate* just now?" After I got over my astonishment, I shot her a sharp glare. "What're you gonna do if we get caught?"

She gave a satisfied smile and a weary reply. "It's mid...night break, so...it's fine."

What the hell, I thought to myself, but I was the one who'd look like an idiot, getting mad at a dunce like her. Nothing I could say would get through to her, no matter what it was, and so I sighed.

"If we get caught, don't bring up my name," I said sternly.

"Of...course not."

When I looked at Yano-san, my eight eyes dripping with mistrust, I saw that she had moved to one of the student seats. Just like during the daytime, she was a girl who lived life at her own tempo.

During lessons we sat in the seats here in the same seating order that we did in the classroom. Naturally, Yano-san followed that order now.

As I closed the lid of the piano with my tail (so that she couldn't play it again), Yano-san asked a friendly question. "Acchi...kun, what music do you lis...ten to?"

"I mean, the normal stuff."

"Like...who?"

She was staring straight at me, so I gave the same answer that I always gave. I offered up the names of artists who everyone at least knew by name, but weren't overly famous, who were on trend but not necessarily household names. There were singer-songwriters who always made the rankings on Tsutaya whenever they put out a new C D, and bands that a few girls in our class were raging over not being able to grab concert tickets for. Yano-san listened, nodding dutifully.

"What about you?" I asked her out of politeness. A second later I found myself thinking that she was probably the sort who listened to quirky things. The kind of music I would never get even if I tried.

I was wrong.

"Well, as...for me..."

She happily divulged the name of just one group. The smile on her face was not her usual smug grin. In fact, her cheeks glowed with pure elation, like she was revealing a secret that she had kept for a long time to a friend. It was the first time I'd ever seen such an expression on her.

I was stunned. The group she had named were not the sort of musicians that one would speak of so confidentially. They were a group that nearly everyone in Japan knew of, who even I had known of since elementary school. The kind of group you would be embarrassed to bring up in serious discussions amongst your friends, who would get you ridiculed if you admitted that you still listened to them. To put it frankly, they were overhyped and super lame.

These were the artists for whom Yano-san confessed her love, as though they were a splendid treasure kept by her and her alone.

I was stunned. "I see," I said, the only suitable reply.

She asked me, "Acchi...kun, do you like them...too?"

"I listen to them now and then. They're all right."

I couldn't pretend I didn't know who they were. Not when, honestly, I still listened to them fairly often.

Yano-san then fervently began explaining the group's appeal to me—the songs, the lyrics, the melodies, the members—all things that I already knew.

As she was explaining which of their albums was the best, her alarm rang from her pocket. I was relieved to know that our time was over, though for a different reason than the night before.

After poking at the phone and silencing the alarm, Yano-san stood and stretched.

"Guess it's...over. I'll go...home and...sleep."

Saying nothing, I opened the door with my tail and allowed her to exit the music room first. I locked the door in the same way I had locked the classroom.

"You can...go ahead," she said to me, as I returned from the black droplets to my original form on the other side of the door. I had no idea how Yano-san returned home, but there was no need for me to know. Following her suggestion, I headed outside.

I wasn't sure whether or not I should be giving some word of parting, but then again, I had only come to fulfill a bargain, so exchanging pleasantries would be weird. That said, it would be just as weird to ignore her. As I sat considering this, she gave that satisfied grin.

"Will...you come here again to...morrow?"

I was silent. I had no intention of coming. And yet, she had given the decision to me, leaving me unable to say as much bluntly.

Unable to answer her question, I decided to simply leap away into the night sky. However, I realized there was still one thing I should say to Yano-san, if nothing else. So, with my back still turned, I tried my best to keep my voice calm. "Sorry for kicking you after gym class."

"Don't ap...ologize for things...that happened during the...day at...night."

Seriously? After I bothered to apologize at all?

Night really was a time best spent alone.

At Night,
I Become a Monster

Thursday
DAY

I THINK THERE ARE REASONS for bullying. Bullying always starts because of some concrete reason. Trivial things like behavior or personal characteristics are a substantial enough reason, at least for the aggressors. It never seems like enough for the one being bullied, obviously. But there's always some rationale, whether it's a good pretext or not—and there's no limit to the evil that can grow within someone once they have the excuse.

In the case of our class, the bullied party was utterly the one at fault and fully in the wrong.

Yano Satsuki had brought her circumstances down on her own shoulders.

I had known Yano since we were second years. Dense, awkward, needlessly loud, with a strange way of speaking, Yano was ridiculed by the boys and some of the girls behind her back. But for some time it just went on like that, with no reason for it to solidify into outright bullying. The members of our class all had a decent amount of sense.

That good sense was swallowed up by a deep tide of righteous anger in the middle of our second year, when a single action of Yano's finally crossed the line.

By this point, it had already become a daily pattern for Yano to rudely impose herself on others and to be shrugged off. That was the basic arrangement between Yano and our classmates. However, there was one person who was the exception for her.

That day, for some reason—which honestly I will never know—she walked up to the desk of one of our classmates, Midorikawa Futaba, who normally came nowhere near her. I really had no idea what kind of relationship they shared. I only thought to myself, *That can't be good.* It was normal for Midorikawa to never actively speak unless she was spoken to, but the fact that Yano wasn't speaking at *all* meant that she had a poor sense of social awareness or something.

However, that assumption was definitely wrong. In fact, Yano most likely had a deep sense of animosity towards Midorikawa. Perhaps she hated Midorikawa for the fact that everyone loved her, even though she never spoke a word, far more than they did Yano herself, who always tried to talk to them.

Whatever the reason, Yano suddenly approached Midorikawa's desk by the window, snatched up the book that she was reading, opened the window, and flung it out into the yard. It was a rainy day. I remember everything, right down to the seating arrangements. Iguchi, sitting in the seat behind Midorikawa, was petrified for several moments.

As far as Yano was concerned, the girl she had targeted was probably also in the wrong. Midorikawa was the class loner and rarely showed her emotions on her face. Now, though, the girl began to cry right there on the spot. She didn't reproach Yano—she simply wept. Later, we learned that the waterlogged book that had been tossed out into the rain was very important to her.

However, the book's significance to Midorikawa was something that we only learned later. That wasn't the reason that the class labeled Yano a villain or why our torment of her became as harsh as it did.

It was because she was smiling. As Midorikawa cried, Yano stood in front of her with that self-satisfied grin, not apologizing. In fact, from that day on, Midorikawa never brought books from home anymore. She only borrowed them from the library, which spurred us on all the more.

When I looked at our class punching bag, I always thought the same thing: her behavior is atrocious. That was the best one could say for Yano.

If she just behaved better, she wouldn't be bullied. That's what I thought the next day as I watched her clean her desk out of the corner of my eye. Since the same thing had happened the day before, I now knew what had happened to the desk. Apparently, someone had covered it in chalk dust from the erasers.

"I heard the monster didn't appear last night."

Kasai was enthusiastic, but I responded with deep caution as we walked down the hall. Deep down, I thought, *Obviously not.* The night before I had headed straight for the school, and after that, I was at the beach, alone.

As we stood in the middle of the hall facing the science lab, I pretended to be deeply interested in this monster story and asked Kasai a vital question.

"Has anyone snapped a pic of it with their phone or anything?"

"They have."

Concealing the pounding of my heart, I replied, "Whoa, awesome."

"Apparently, none of the pictures came out, though. So I still don't believe it."

I prayed that he would just lose interest there. But it was interesting to learn that my monstrous form apparently couldn't be caught on film. Suddenly, I recalled *Pom Poko* and the plan that the spirits in the movie enacted. At any rate, this was advantageous to me. If I was immune to being recorded, I could go wherever I wanted.

When we arrived in the science lab, our good-natured science teacher was already writing on the blackboard. I followed after Kasai and took my seat without any overt greeting. The seating order from the classroom wasn't used in the science lab. We sat in groups of six at long tables arranged into even rows, sorted by attendance number. I was in the "A" row, closest to the door, my spot shielding the seats occupied by the boisterous Kasai and company one row behind.

I didn't hate our lessons in the science lab. The other five students in my group weren't the type to stand out or cause trouble; I mostly enjoyed their company. As long as I did my job well in the group leader role I was forced into, class went smoothly.

Of course, when you considered not just myself, but our whole class, arranging the seating this way was probably all the better.

Kasai loudly said something or other to me, but just as I was replying, his gaze flicked away towards the entrance of the room. I slowly turned around, saw who it was, and then returned to my conversation with Kasai.

Midorikawa was walking slowly through the entrance. As always, she carried nothing more than what she needed for class, along with a book from the library. The seat she was headed for was on the window side, second group from the back. Motoda was already there, asleep with his face against the table. Midorikawa took the seat diagonal from him, opened up her textbook and notebook, and then her library book. She sat up straight and tall as always.

After a short while, the bell rang. The teacher paused what he was writing on the board and turned around. "Let's begin," he said with a smile, accompanied by a command of "All rise!" from the class representative.

With timing so perfect that it almost seemed planned, the instant that we all stood, there was a click and then a rattling sound from the door at the front of the lab. It shook within its frame. I wasn't startled—I'd anticipated this and put myself on guard. Even though there was no need to, and honestly, no *reason* to, whoever had entered the room last had locked the door.

With a look of exasperation on his face, the teacher instructed the girl sitting closest to the door to unlock it. The girl reluctantly opened the door, her disinterest plain.

On the other side of the door stood Yano, blinking rapidly. Without saying a word, she headed quickly for her seat. Chalk-colored dust shaded some of her hair. She didn't appear to have noticed.

Throughout the lab, you could feel a coldness brimming in everyone's hearts, save for the teacher's. The sound of Yano's shoes tapping across the floor resounded, and until she stood at her assigned place, everyone stared forward, waiting in silence.

When the teacher's second call to begin finally rang out, the tense atmosphere seemed to defuse. I didn't look Yano's way, but she was probably smiling, as she always did. She was at the same back table as Midorikawa.

Yano had been the perpetrator here, so the contempt she inspired was only to be expected. After all, you reap what you sow.

On the other hand, one had to wonder how Midorikawa felt; she never showed her emotions on her face. The very fact that she said nothing made the rest of us worry that she might actually hate this seating arrangement, which intensified the hostility towards Yano all the more.

Yano had probably arrived late because she had been asleep somewhere during our twenty-minute break. She could always be found napping in some relatively quiet place around then. I was the only one who knew why she was always so sleep-deprived, but I had nothing pertinent to say in her defense. That too was all her own doing.

The beginning of class only offered a brief distraction from thinking about Yano, interrupted by Yano running up to the front of the classroom after I and the other group leaders collected the handouts for our groups from the front desk. As I began to wonder if she hadn't gotten a handout, she told the teacher that she had forgotten her textbook and then asked if she could go and get it.

The teacher wearily responded with something twisted. "We can't waste any more time today. Just share with your neighbor."

Saying nothing, Yano returned to the back of the lab, a satisfied smile on her face. Without waiting for her to take her seat, class began. I looked straight ahead towards the blackboard. I didn't so much as glance back. Even without looking, I could picture exactly what was going on. There was no need to see it with my own eyes.

One of the best things about science class, I thought, was probably that Yano never had to cross my line of sight for the whole class period. I couldn't shield myself from any noises that came from behind us, of course, but there was nothing to be done about that.

"Stop that," I warned the girl sitting beside me, who was busy gawking back, her attention caught by the noise. At my warning, perhaps realizing that others could see what she was doing, Iguchi quickly put her eyes back down to her paper. I was relieved that she wouldn't draw any more attention to herself than she already had.

Yano's standing in our class had been wrought both by the members of our class and by Yano herself, but naturally there were those among us who did not actively display any ill will towards her.

The worst offender was Iguchi. Compared to Yano, Iguchi was friendly with everyone, a kind girl who would lavish anyone but Yano with smiles. Though Iguchi tried to hide it—which was probably the wisest decision, I knew—she constantly kept an eye on Yano when she was being bullied, fretting over whether the others might be overdoing it.

That said, she was still on the class's side rather than Yano's. While I was usually content to ignore Yano, I couldn't help but notice Iguchi's nervous face. Honestly, it might be easier for her if someone else definitively decided her side for her. All that dithering must have caused her a ton of stress. Not that it was any of my business, though.

Science class proceeded normally, without incident. If something was happening where I couldn't see it, then I didn't need to know about it. All I needed to do was sit with my group members and focus on learning about hereditary traits.

It's not like things ever get too out of hand in these situations. At the very worst, sometimes people's belongings were damaged, or people got a bit hurt. The most that usually happened in our class was that something belonging to Yano got soaked or dirtied. She had suffered a fair few injuries, sure, but they were always total accidents, brought on by her own clumsiness. Nobody's fault but her own. There was never any violence that anyone could see.

Everyone in class was clever enough to make sure.

Thus, what happened after science class really couldn't be defined as an "incident." Way too strong a word. Things just got a little out of hand, that's all.

Yano was walking several meters ahead of me in the hallway, en route back to the classroom. There were a number of other students walking in the same direction in the space between me and her. This distance was not by chance. I had slackened my pace just a little, so that even if she were to suddenly stumble again, no one could say that I'd kicked her. So far, the plan was a success. I felt pretty comfortable with how far apart we were.

...And that was why I grew careless.

I was talking with the other boys about a TV show that had aired the day before. Something that Yano had been juggling back and forth went tumbling out of her hands. The tri-colored object—blue, black, and white—was more than likely an eraser.

I caught this moment in the dead center of my sight. And though it was faint, I let slip a small "Oh." That was no good. My voice drew the gaze of everyone else around.

Yano didn't crouch down today. There was no need for her to do so.

I'm sure that she didn't mean much by it, but...

It was Iguchi.

Straying apart from a group of girls she'd been walking with, Iguchi found herself right behind Yano. Perhaps unintentionally, perhaps reflexively, she picked the eraser up off the ground.

Don't do it! I thought, but it was too late to stop her.

Iguchi was probably stunned herself. Maybe she only realized what she had done once she'd already done it. She locked eyes with Yano, who turned around and froze for several seconds.

Ignoring someone is like a habit or custom. At first, you have to do it intentionally, but as you become accustomed to it, it becomes natural to act like they aren't even there. Eventually your body ignores them all on its own, like it's second nature.

Iguchi had yet to acquire the habit of ignoring Yano. On the contrary, she was a slave to a different kind of habit—the common courtesy of picking up something that someone else has dropped. That was the kind of heart she had, a natural kindness that made little gestures like that as easy as breathing.

Thus—unfortunately—she happened to pick up the eraser that had fallen right in front of her.

Iguchi was still frozen, eye-to-eye with Yano. Without thinking, I stopped walking as well.

Yano held her right hand outstretched stupidly to Iguchi, with a lively "Thank...you!"

Then she snatched the eraser from Iguchi's hand, turned on her heel, and walked on.

From behind Yano's back, the girls of our class stared at the two of them. Their eyes suggested they had just spotted yet another cockroach. I have no idea what expression was on Iguchi's face, but you didn't have to think very hard to know why she blurted out a thin "It's not like that" just a moment later.

A momentary silence fell over the hallway—a short grace period for Iguchi to make some sort of excuse. However, she stayed silent. She probably couldn't come up with anything to say.

And then the spell was broken. Time began to flow once more. The girls up ahead began walking towards the classroom, discussing something or other, and we followed behind them. Yano proceeded at her own pace, as always. She resumed her juggling, not much caring how many times she'd failed at it.

And Iguchi just stood there as everyone left her behind.

I wondered if she would be okay.

It was unfortunate, but while I worried for her, it was nothing that I was about to obsess over.

It happened after school that day. After Yano, as always, left the classroom with a "Bye, ev...eryone," without stopping to talk with anyone.

That was when the girls of our class surrounded Iguchi.

It happened on the far end of classroom, so I couldn't hear what they were saying. All I know is that Iguchi was vehemently denying something, looking as though she was about to cry.

This sure went south, I thought to myself, as I prepared to leave. She messed up.

Not about to step in between the girls or anything clever like that, I elected to leave the classroom with Kasai and the others.

After we stepped out into the hall and passed by another classroom, Kasai tilted his head.

"Did Igu-chan do somethin'?"

Right, Kasai hadn't been there when it all went down.

"Iguchi happened to pick up something that Yano dropped," I explained, trying as best as I possibly could to imply that Iguchi was not the one at fault. Hearing that, the other guys laughed. "Gross! Yano cooties!"

The corners of Kasai's mouth dipped. "What, seriously?"

He seemed displeased. Probably not over what Iguchi had done, I reasoned, but simply from hearing Yano's name. Yet as soon as we arrived at our shoe lockers, his temperament completely shifted. "Oh, that reminds me," he said, with an air that suggested he had suddenly remembered something far more interesting. "Wanna go see the baseball clubroom?"

"The baseball club? Why?"

At my frank question, Kasai began to laugh. "What? I thought you were the one who told me about it, Acchi. Guess I was wrong. Anyway, apparently a window got broken in the baseball clubroom. Last night."

"Last night?"

"Yeah, some guy probably threw a rock through it as a prank or something."

Night. A prank. The baseball club window.

No way. It couldn't be.

"Hm, what's with that face, Acchi? Are you the culprit?"

Alarmed at Kasai's grin, I quickly forced my expression into one of vague displeasure.

"Like hell I am. I was just wonderin' who'd be that stupid."

An eerie sense of premonition was spreading throughout my whole body. I got the feeling I knew exactly who that stupid criminal was. *She* hadn't been there when I arrived at the classroom the night before.

Was she really off just laying a little frog to rest? Could she actually have been off seeking vengeance for it along the way?

Nervously, though there was really no reason to be nervous, we decided to change from our indoor shoes to our athletic shoes and go check out the baseball clubroom.

The baseball clubroom adjoined the soccer and rugby clubrooms, down at the far end of the wide field shared by various sports clubs. From a distance, they all looked like one big massive block. As we approached, we could see a sheet of cardboard tacked on to the window frame. A club member was coming out of the room at that very moment, someone who happened to be a friend of Kasai's. After we hollered at him, he explained that their club adviser had put the cardboard up that morning.

Though we'd come with no great expectations, our enthusiasm waned, and we decided to head home. We greeted our other classmates as we passed them by, received the customary "Later," "See ya," or "Yeah" in return, but just as we crossed the entrance, our eyes stopped on a small girl who was exiting, her eyes to the ground.

Her spirit was broken. There was no other way to describe her. As I considered how to address the girl, mindful of the eyes of the other girls around, Kasai waved his hand.

"Later, Igu-chan!"

Hearing Kasai's lively voice, Iguchi weakly lifted her head and smiled, replying with a "Later" that suggested nothing less than utter exhaustion.

The feeble little smile on her face was pure heartbreak.

But still, that was Kasai for you. When he waved at her again, saying, "See ya!" as though he knew nothing about earlier, Iguchi's strange smile deepened a little more.

As we walked away, I told Kasai, "You really shouldn't bother her like that."

Kasai replied, laughing, "It's not like Igu-chan is seriously friends with that girl."

If only I could be like Kasai, I thought—but in the end, I still did nothing.

Thursday NIGHT

THOUGH I KNEW it wouldn't do any good, I was livid with Yano-san. If she hadn't been doing that weird juggling thing in the hall, Iguchi-san wouldn't have been berated so cruelly. However, the reason that I headed to school again that evening wasn't just to criticize her for that, no. There was something else on my mind: the baseball club. On the off chance she really had broken that window, then that act was far more grave. It was downright criminal.

When I arrived at the school and slipped through the back door of the classroom, Yano was digging through the trash can near the blackboard for something. Unsure of how to call out to a girl who was elbow-deep in garbage, I decided to wait until she noticed me.

When Yano, clutching something thin in both hands with an *Aha*, finally noticed the monster at the back of the classroom, she cried out with a vapid "Wuh-hoh!"

"Yo," I greeted.

"...Look...at that. You...came," she said, flapping the object, which seemed to be some notepads, around in her hand.

I had thought at the very least that I would be met with that usual satisfied grin of hers, but she couldn't seem to care less about the fact that I was here. It left me feeling a little down. Not that I was looking forward to her smile, or anything.

Just as I thought, *Enough, I'm going home,* and began to disassemble my form, she asked me a strange question. "Acchi...kun, are you a Fire...ball type? Or a Frizz type?"

Fireball? Frizz? Was she talking about games?

"You mean for fire magic?" I said. "I prefer Incendio."

"What's...that?"

"From Harry Potter."

"Wow... Then can...you do...that?"

"Huh?"

"Can...you breathe...fire?"

"Sure can't."

She looked disheartened at my response. What was that face about?

I was the one who ought to be put out, I thought. But when I considered Yano-san's disappointment, I recalled the rumors that Kasai had mentioned, about a kaiju appearing. Since she knew that the rumors were about me, she must have figured that if I was a kaiju, I could probably breathe fire or something.

"What d'you need fire for anyway?"

"To burn...this. Any...way, let's go...to the...roof."

As usual, she exited the classroom without waiting for my reply. Left without much choice, I locked the door in my usual way and followed behind. I was honestly a bit impressed by how conscientious I was every time.

By the time I made it out to the hallway, I found that my free-spirited classmate had already started towards the stairs, not waiting for me. My self-admiration turned to exasperation. The fact that I followed her was not conscientiousness but softhearted foolishness.

I prepared a Shadow clone just in case, but we arrived at the roof without incident.

As I unlocked the rooftop door and we stepped outside, I was struck by a crisp breeze. Though I had been here the night before last, I had forgotten how good a feeling it was being on the rooftop in the middle of the night. One got the feeling that the sky might just swallow us whole.

"People shouldn't...smoke," said Yano-san, pointing at a cigarette butt that was rolling by.

"Well, I mean..." I paused. "It's no big deal, as long as they don't get caught."

"But it's...bad for the...body."

She was right, of course, but it was weird to hear something so sensible and mature out of Yano-san. The ones who came up here to smoke were probably the ones who kicked off the bullying against you, I wanted to say. But there was no need for it, so I kept my mouth shut.

"Now...then, show...me some...fire."

"Uh, no, I just told you that I can't."

"Have you...tried?"

Now that she asked me, not only had I not tried it, I hadn't even considered it.

"Just try...it...one...time. Oh, ac...tually, I've never tried it... either, so I'll try...too. Go!"

She placed the two notebooks on the ground and held out her hands like she was trying to gather up energy. Her arms trembling, she muttered again and again: "Go...! Go...!" For some reason, partway through, she appeared to stop breathing. I watched her for a while, thinking about how stupid she looked. At length, she seemed to accept her own powerlessness and sat down, grumbling. "Guess I...can't." Her shoulders heaved, as though she had been putting in some real, serious effort.

"Okay... Now it's your...turn, Acchi...kun."

"Huh?"

I flicked my eyes away from her hopeful gaze and observed the two notebooks. Both had been scribbled all over in magic marker. What was written all over them were not childish little insults like "Big Dummy" or "Stupid Idiot." This stuff was nasty. Their covers were scrawled with enough vitriol to deeply wound anyone who read it, not just Yano-san.

"If fire does come out, can I burn those?"

"That's...fine. I've al...ready used them...all up, so I'd put... them a...side."

Even if she hadn't, would she really ever use them again, the way they were now?

"I threw...them away, but...I thought it... might be better to... burn them."

Ah, so it wasn't that someone else had thrown them in the trash; she'd done it herself.

I wondered how long they'd been defaced. I highly doubted that whoever did it had the courtesy to choose a notebook she'd already filled.

While I stood there thinking, there came a demand of "Hurry...up!"

Yano-san had moved some distance away from the notebooks, clearly believing in my power. I had my doubts, but those notebooks looked so pitiful. If I could honor them with a proper cremation, I thought that I might as well try.

If I could make a Shadow, then why not fire, too? If I said I wasn't a little optimistic about my chances, I'd be lying.

I visualized it, the same way I had the night before.

In order to breathe fire, I needed to store up enough energy to make my whole body vibrate. Then, I had to make the black drops inside of my monstrous form crank like an engine and heat up. Then, the droplets had to ignite, gathering up into a big flame, which I would spit from my mouth.

Suddenly, I was assailed by a bright light shining in front of me.

"Gaaah! It's...hot!"

The flame that flew from my mouth was exactly as large as I had imagined. So large it came dangerously close to catching Yano-san's uniform. Quickly, I breathed in, picturing a sudden end to the heat, a re-absorption of the burning droplets. As I did, the flames returned to my body, stopping just short of injuring her.

The moonlight-tempered darkness returned to the rooftop, and there in the midst of it sat two notebooks burned to a crisp.

The two of us looked at each other.

"Whoa! Wow! That's a...mazing!"

Yano-san stared fixedly at me as she walked from the edge of the rooftop back to where I stood. Inadvertently, I stared right back with all eight of my eyes.

"No way," I said.

I had hoped, at least a little bit, that I might be able to do something like that, but I never believed that I actually could.

I totally *was* a kaiju.

If I wasn't careful with this fire-breathing, I could set the whole town ablaze, just like a real kaiju.

I could still feel the flame kindling within my body. Excitement burned with its own fire deep inside my heart.

"That's so...cool, Acchi-kun. How'd you...do it?"

How *had* I done it?

"I just, like, imagined how I thought it would feel, and then I did it," I tried to explain as Yano-san timidly approached. She stared at me with the wide-eyed look of someone facing down a monster.

"With the power of...imagination, any...thing is...possible," she said.

"Power of imagination?"

Was there really such a thing? A real power, like a wizard or sorcerer's?

Yano-san gave the burnt notebooks a powerful kick, and they scattered into black flecks. Apparently, I had burned them completely to ash.

After scattering the ashes to her satisfaction, Yano-san took a step back and once again stared at me. I wondered if she might be afraid, knowing that I was a genuine fire-breathing monster, but that was probably wrong. I realized then that the color in her eyes was a completely different hue from what they'd shown before. It was the color of envy.

She really was a strange girl. Who would want to be a monster? I doubted that I could really do *anything* I wanted, like she'd implied, anyway. But then...what if I *could*...?

As I pictured it, a whisper of fear ran through me.

But just what was I so afraid of...?

"...Say... Acchi...kun."

I was afraid that she might come to say something like, *If you can do anything, then rescue me.*

So I interrupted her. "That reminds me, Yano-san." It was time to finally finish the business that had brought me here in the first place. "Do you know about what happened with the baseball club?"

"Hm? What...happened?"

"Seems like someone smashed their clubroom window."

"Right, some...one was saying...that."

"Yeah, so..."

I had only spoken two words when Yano-san suddenly began to cackle. She kicked at the ashes again, her feet loudly thumping on the ground. Just when I was starting to wonder if she'd finally lost it, she pointed at me.

"And you thought...I was...the culprit."

Though she was in fact right on the mark, I was startled that she could guess it.

"Uh, well, yeah. I thought, maybe."

"I'd never...do something like...that."

For the first time that night, she showed me that smug grin.

"If I got...revenge for my...self, I would be...just like...them."

Just like them—by which she meant she would be just the same as Motoda. Which further meant that, as far as Yano-san was concerned, that was a bad thing.

"If not for yourself, then what about for the frog?"

"I...wouldn't. I have no...idea what that...little one would have...wanted. I wouldn't... do something so...stupid."

I was lost for words. For so many reasons, but mostly because I was stunned that Yano-san would ever think that carefully about her own actions. *If that were the case, why didn't she always exercise a bit more self-awareness,* I wondered. And as I wondered, I realized that the insults written on those notebooks might be a little bit off the mark.

Not that I had the slightest intention of validating Yano-san, of course.

"Ah, seems like...you still...doubt me."

"I mean, uh, not really."

"Well then."

Yano-san grinned again, not smugly, but as though she were plotting something.

"Let's...catch the true...cul...prit."

"Hm?"

The true culprit? That was the first time I'd ever heard a phrase like that outside of a detective manga.

"Acchi...kun, are...you a...Detective Conan fan or a...Kindaichi...fan?"

"I prefer Neuro. Anyway, it's not like I doubt you. There's no point in searching for the true culprit just to prove me wrong."

"I like...Yako-chan."

"Oh, cool."

So she was a Jump reader. I found myself getting more and more surprised every time I found out this strange girl shared something in common with me.

"Why don't you...want to look?"

"I mean, it was obviously just a random idiot throwing a rock or something."

"Oh, I see, so...the broken window was...on the road...side."

Once she said that, I realized what it was that I had just assumed, not even thinking. The broken window *was* on the field side. That I needed Yano-san to point that out, even though I had been the one to see the broken window, was embarrassing.

"Anyway, let's...go and see the...scene of the...crime."

I didn't see any reason for Yano-san to be so enthusiastic, but when I heaved a heavy, obvious sigh, she merely replied, "It's im... portant to breathe...deeply." Oh, forget it.

"Won't you get caught if you go out on the field?"

"It's mid...night break, so it's...fine. I'll stick along the...wall, which should block views from...the outside, too. Acchi...kun, you can...hide yourself in the...shadows."

"Wait, I'm coming, too?"

"Oh yeah, I...hear it's gonna... rain to...morrow."

As usual, she wasn't listening to a word I said.

If she was going to ignore me, then I really should have just ignored her, too. I got the feeling that someone somewhere was condemning me as a softie.

If it rained tomorrow, that meant that Yano-san might not make her nighttime visit to school. I prepared a Shadow and then headed down the stairs back off the roof. Today would be the last day. I could do her at least this much of a favor for now.

Along the way I became aware of the sound of Yano-san's indoor shoes tapping on the floor. I warned her about it, and she smiled dimly. She removed the shoes, stuck them on her hands, and then proceeded to clap them together, which meant I had to warn her *again*. Was she a little kid?

As I considered where the safest exit from the building might be, a question occurred to me. "How do you usually get into the building?"

"I come...through the front...entrance from the...main gate."

"I don't mean during school hours."

Seemingly uninterested in my clarification, Yano-san walked right on ahead of me. I quickly sent the Shadow down first to make sure that no one was around. Thankfully, we were able to make it to the first floor without running into any guards. The guard room was located in another structure that adjoined to the main hallway. Next to the front door that the teachers used as an entrance was the guest reception area. Now that I thought about it, the student entrance didn't face out onto any conspicuous places like the fields or the courtyard, so that might be fine.

As I pondered, we arrived at the entrance. Of course, though I was perfectly fine barefoot, Yano-san would need to switch from her indoor shoes to her sneakers.

I waited nervously as she rummaged boldly and noisily through the shoe box. She switched her shoes on the spot and proceeded straight for the closed door. *Wouldn't the door be locked?* I wondered, but neither Yano-san nor the door itself cared about my concerns.

By which I mean, the door was open.

Why?

"Let's...go."

"Why was that unlocked?" I asked.

"Be...cause it was un...locked when I...got here."

"That's ridiculous."

Ignoring my retort, that idiot plodded out towards the field. When I pointed out that no matter how far we were from the guard room, there was still a chance that they might spot us out on patrol, Yano-san only replied, "Keep it...down." She crouched low and stuck close to the side of the building. I wondered whether I shouldn't just stop her mouth up with black specks but stopped myself before I could try. It would turn into a pretty dreadful ordeal if I accidentally suffocated her, and since I hadn't yet made physical contact with any human in my monstrous form, I had no idea what might happen. I couldn't even begin to think about how I'd cope if the black droplets swallowed her up the same way they did me.

We crept low along the building walls, passing behind the gym until we approached the cluster of clubrooms. Poised between the trees that grew up against the fence, we ascertained the location of the broken window. Obviously, it hadn't magicked itself back to normal; the carboard sheet was still fixed in place.

"It's hard to...see it from...here."

"Even if we got closer, it's not like we could fix it or anything. Let's go back."

"A perpe...trator always re...turns to the scene of...the crime."

"Even if they did come back, I don't think they'd come back right *now*."

"You like Harry...Potter, right?" She leaned back against the fence, clearly confident in her words. I resisted the urge to rip my own hair out (so to speak) and sat down on the ground, resigned.

"We've got them at home, anyway. My parents bought them because they were popular."

"Oh...so you're more...of a DVD type than...a movie theater type?"

"...I prefer the books."

Even though that was true, and even though there was no reason anyone ought to be embarrassed by it, for some reason, I still hesitated to admit it. I'd never anticipated anyone in class asking me what kind of books I read, so I hadn't taken the time to prepare a sufficiently appropriate answer.

Yano-san looked shocked. "Wow!"

That girl was way too loud. "Come on, quiet down..."

"I can't...believe you've read...books that big. Are you...a big reader, then?"

"I mean, maybe a little. Not that much."

Of course I had read all of Harry Potter. The books weren't hard reads, and they were fun, too. Knowing how worked up she got when it came to talking about her interests, though, I didn't elaborate.

"I can't imagine being...interested in...books."

Just as I was thinking that the girl in front of me did not seem like much of a reader, she confessed to it herself. Wait, *confessed* was probably a little too in line with Yano-san's detective game. It was more like an admission. One that she had made of her own free will.

"I wonder if I should...watch the movies. Books are...all full of letters, and my eyes...get tired. And they...take so long. I...know that there are...people who can get...through a book just like... that, but manga are way...quicker to read. And more...fun."

"There are novels that are fun, too."

Crap, I thought. I hadn't meant to get into a debate with her, but she just shook her head, saying, "I...doubt that."

I was shocked at myself. For the first time in these last three nights, I was glad that she was the only one here. The late hour, being a monster...it must have all been getting to me. Here, now, I had asserted my own interests. During the day, I never would have made that stand. I just would have gone with the flow.

"I feel...like you...would just get...stupider...if all...you read... is letters."

Yano-san's words floated out into the air as though they were a song.

I couldn't help but feel those words were directed towards a specific one of our classmates. Come to think of it, Yano-san's midnight breaks or whatever, all this sneaking into the school, it was directly related to that one girl who did nothing but read books.

Midorikawa Futaba.

What did Yano-san think of her ever since that incident? I can't say that I wasn't curious to know, but I had no interest in sticking my nose into problems that I couldn't solve, so I didn't ask.

We remained there until the alarm rang on Yano-san's phone, but the true culprit never showed. I told her that I would search for them later, so she could shut off the alarm, but she let it ring all the way through.

"If you get caught, I know nothing about this, *seriously*."

"You're so per...sistent. There are...guards here, so...it's fine."

But that *wasn't* fine. Also, I had no idea if there were any teachers who ever came in after dark, but if any of *them* caught her, the consequences would be far more dire than just being caught by a guard. I had kept silent about the possibility at first, since I knew that no matter how much I warned her, she wouldn't listen...but if she wanted *me* to come with her, then...

"Worry...wart. You're such a...worrywart."

I was annoyed at the teasing. And so, as I faced the entrance, sticking to the wall, I decided to finally lodge one complaint that I had been putting aside.

"Yano-san, why are you always so thoughtless? Why'd you go and yank that eraser from Iguchi-san like that, after she picked it up for you so nicely?"

"Don't talk about...the daytime," she said dismissively, not looking at me. Gazing at her from behind just then, I felt the droplets of my body grow restless, like hackles standing on end.

Any longer and that restless motion would have become something unspeakable.

"I'm...sure that..."

It was only because Yano-san began to speak that the trembling of my body settled. I was a monster who listened closely to what others had to say.

"...Igu-chan is a...nice girl."

Really? Was that all she had to say? Obviously, I knew that already.

We shared no more words until we reached the school gates, which for some reason were open like normal.

I gave her the simplest word of parting and left the school behind. As I leapt up into the sky and headed for the sea, I saw Yano-san below me, climbing atop a bicycle near the gates.

I worried a little about whether she would be okay all alone at this time of night, but she was grinning as always, so I let her be.

My anger at her had drifted somewhere far away without me ever noticing.

Friday
DAY

*Y*ANO'S BULLYING was due in large part to the sense of unity that our class shared.

The next morning, just like Yano had said, it started to rain.

On rainy days, I walked to school with an umbrella. To be honest, I would rather have ridden my bike like usual, but if any teachers spotted me wielding an umbrella while riding I would be chewed out. That'd be a major pain, and no one ever went around wearing ponchos, and I wasn't about to be the one dweeb using one.

Walking to school took a fair while longer, but since I no longer required sleep, I could wake up early and take my time eating breakfast and get to school without issue. I was much hungrier than usual that morning and ended up eating four slices of toast. I wondered if it had anything to do with last night's fire breathing.

I arrived at school after a relatively easy commute, my walk scored by the sound of my music player. It was full of popular tunes. On rainy days, some students had their parents drive them to school, and there were others like me who preferred to walk, so more students than usual came skirting in just before the bell. I, on the other hand, arrived much earlier than I predicted, while the entryway was fairly empty. Still outside, I folded up my umbrella and shook off the raindrops before heading in.

Yano stood there, drenched from head to toe.

I hadn't anticipated this encounter. My expression was probably a bit strained. When I looked at Yano, who was busy wringing out her skirt, she gave me that satisfied grin. "Good mor...ning."

Yano offering pointless greetings to her classmates was the norm. Even so, I stood there for just a moment, struck dumb. The gods of fortune must have truly been on my side, given that none of our other classmates were present.

"Some...one took my um...brella."

Before she could even finish informing me of this tragic circumstance, I returned to my senses. I averted my gaze and successfully carried myself to our class's shoe boxes. Despite my ignoring her, I caught Yano still grinning in the corner of my eye. Just as I was thinking to myself how truly strange she was, I heard a voice from behind us.

"Good morning, Yano-san. Why don't you come with me to the nurse's office? I'll lend you a towel."

"Thank...you very...much."

Classic Noto, always on the ball. I silently thanked her. With her arrival, both my wishes had been granted. Not only did I avoid having to talk to Yano, the girl was going to stop dripping everywhere. Thank the heavens above.

When I arrived at the classroom, sure enough, over half of the seats remained empty. Two cliques had already arrived: Takao's group of boys, with their loud voices, and Nakagawa's group of girls, who had been the ones to attack Iguchi yesterday. All of them bubbled with talk of how they had destroyed a classmate's umbrella. I put my umbrella into the stand and my bag into my locker, pretending not to listen.

I worried that just sitting silently at my desk might be bad for my health, so I turned and discussed a show that had aired the night before with my neighbor, Kudou. It was a garden-variety romantic drama with very few twists. It was popular, and I had been watching since the second episode. Honestly, I still didn't get what was so great about it, but other people seemed to be moved by it—and I wasn't opposed to having a close female friend rave about it and show me her full, double-toothed smile.

Kasai arrived after a short while, giving a spectacular greeting that reached every corner of the room. I raised a hand to him as well. Since Takao had already enthusiastically confessed to the divine punishment he had dispensed, I decided to chime in, too. I picked my moment, waiting until Kasai was passing by my seat to take his bag to his locker.

"Y'know, she was totally soaked back at the entrance," I said.

A laugh erupted. Thank goodness. It was weird for such a rainy day, but everyone seemed to be in slightly higher spirits than usual. Perhaps it was because the windows were closed tight in order to keep the room from getting drenched. It made the room feel a bit like a secret clubhouse of sorts. We felt that sense of unity stronger than ever.

I had previously heard the teachers say that our class was a good one, without any problems. That was, of course, as long as you turned a blind eye to the matter of Yano, but it was clear that was exactly what the teachers were inclined to do. There were some rough guys like Motoda, and some minor violations of school regulations now and then, but there were no reports of violence or matters that would concern the police. On the whole, we were a good, well-disciplined group.

"I just wish Midorikawa had seen it," said Takao.

"Right?" I laughed.

Of course, I had no intention of arguing that Yano was the victim here. Yano had brought this situation down upon herself. It was her own conduct that incited this bullying. What could one say but that Yano was the one in the wrong here for going after Midorikawa?

That said, the reason that she'd made a mistake by harassing Midorikawa was not simply because Midorikawa was beloved by everyone.

"Morning!"

I turned to look as Kasai greeted someone at the back of the classroom with a wide smile. Midorikawa herself had just arrived. She replied with her usual "Mm," and we responded by casually greeting her back. It was impossible to discern what internal rules governed the number of times Midorikawa might nod or the timing of such, but she gave one more "Mm" for good measure and headed to her seat.

He probably didn't want the rest of us to notice, but Kasai had just received his own individual "Mm" from Midorikawa and was grinning even wider than before. It was a different type of smile than the one he gave anyone else—that much was painfully clear to everyone.

Without a doubt, Kasai was the heart and soul of our class. In the center of our class, which had developed an all-around enmity for Yano, was Kasai.

That said, Kasai had never done anything to Yano. The only connection between the two was that Kasai was the nucleus of the class and that he was unhappy with her. The greatest tragedy for Yano was the fact that everyone was aware of that one tiny thing.

A shared sense of unity.

"Mor...ning."

Out of the corner of my eye I caught sight of Yano, wrapped in a slightly large tracksuit that she had probably borrowed from the nurse's office. She greeted everyone with a smug grin upon her face, but no one responded. On the contrary, Takao clicked his tongue loudly. That was odd in and of itself.

Unconcerned, Yano placed her bag down on her desk, a smile still upon her face. She took her seat, only to stand straight back up with a soft shriek. I looked over and saw that the bottom portion of her red tracksuit was soaked. Someone must have poured water on her seat before I arrived. After staring at it in confusion,

Yano wiped her chair with the sleeve of the borrowed tracksuit and sat back down.

I doubt Takao's group did it. If they had, they'd have done it while announcing their involvement with the umbrella incident. The perpetrator was someone else.

With the exception of a single individual, all of the members of our class were humans, day and night. They didn't all think and act in the same way, like some kind of hive mind. We all had our own individual attitudes toward Yano, but in general, everyone fell into one of three categories.

The first type were the ones who harmed her overtly, those who relished in it. Motoda and Takao and the girls who had harassed Iguchi the day before, they were all this type.

The second were the ones who clearly didn't like Yano but only bothered to show it whenever she came near them or engaged in some more subtle type of antagonism. My neighbor, Kudou, was of this type. The majority of the class fell into this category.

The third type were the ones who thought that Yano was in the wrong but who mainly just ignored her, not going out of our way to do anything about it, such as Iguchi, Kasai, and myself. We were a rare breed, our numbers few.

With the exception of Yano and Midorikawa, the rest of our class could be divided up into those three categories. The one who had wet Yano's seat was most likely one of the first two types. It was the type-twos who were probably the most bothersome for Yano, acting only when their enemy couldn't see them, unlike the brazen Motoda and Takao.

None of us were about to go nosing around for the culprit. There was a shared sentiment between us that we were all in it together and an implicit agreement that, unless the culprit should out themselves, no one was going to bother searching for them. Now that I thought about it, there had been a teacher during our first year who said that ratting out a friend was worse than bullying. Whether or not one thought that was true was a matter of personal opinion.

When the bell finally came, everyone began filing into their seats. As I thought, the classroom was a little noisier than usual, but when I looked around at what seats were still empty, I realized: Iguchi wasn't there.

That was unusual. She always came to school early, carrying on hushed conversations with the girls she was closest to. I was pretty sure that I'd seen her brought to school by car on rainy days, but even so, she was still late.

As I chatted with Kudou about which high schools we wanted to attend, I began to grow worried about Iguchi. Was she that torn up about what happened the day before?

When the last bell rang, two latecomers arrived. Motoda came running in from morning practice, and Midorikawa had returned from the library, book in hand. They both took their seats, and just behind them came the teacher. Our class representative gave the usual commands.

The word *truant* floated through my head. Just then, I heard a small voice say, "Pardon me." Iguchi entered from the door at the front of the room and took her seat three places in front of me.

Seeing the swaying of the Totoro key chain that always hung from Iguchi's bag put me at ease, but at the same time, I understood—she had likely arrived just now on purpose. She was probably afraid that she would be harangued again before class, the way she had yesterday afternoon.

"Today's duties are assigned to Adachi and Iguchi."

Just as I was managing to catch my breath after sitting back down again, my name was called. Right, we did have to deal with those today. Whenever our class had to relocate during first period, whoever was on duty had the key to the classroom handed over to them. Today's first period was music. Iguchi was busy taking her textbooks out of her bag, so I stood up to handle it. "I got it, I got it," I told her, going up to take the key. I said it twice, so as not to seem like I was showing off.

When I turned around, Iguchi extended a quiet thanks, so low she was nearly mouthing the words. I returned the sentiment with a smile, and she hurriedly continued preparing for class. As I passed by her seat, my eyes were still on her for some reason.

That was when it happened.

Iguchi slammed her desk loudly, as though she had a spasm or something.

For a moment, all the air stopped flowing in the classroom, until Kasai joked, "Well, that was startling," and the incident was quickly forgotten. Thus, I was probably the only one who had noticed it.

The reason that the top of her desk had been raised, and then come down with such a sound, was that she had slammed it shut with violent force.

As I sat down at my seat in the back of the room, key in hand, my heart raced violently, making a terrible sound in my ears.

What *was* that?

I had seen it.

Iguchi had been reaching for a notebook that she had left in her desk. Then, when she saw the front of it, she immediately slammed her hands down to try to hide it.

There was no mistaking it. Her notebook looked exactly like the ones I'd burned for Yano the night before. There were terrible words written all over the front of Iguchi's notebook in magic marker.

Sense. Of. Unity.

Even after homeroom ended and we exited the classroom, I could not quell the pounding of my heart.

"What's up, Acchi? Your stomach hurt?"

Though I had tried the whole day to conceal how rattled I'd been that morning, Kasai began to fuss over me during cleanup time. So that no one would make any false assumptions, I put a weary look on my face. "I'm just tired of all these class duties. How come we only ever seem to have music or gym or whatever when it's my turn?"

Iguchi had been visibly depressed all day, but it didn't seem that anyone was fussing much about her. In all likelihood, one or all of the girls who had harassed her the day before were guilty of defacing her notebook. They all seemed to be avoiding her now. Likely everyone else was aware of how they had been bothering her, assumed the cause, and thought nothing of it.

In other words, no one bothered comforting her because everyone felt the same way: If she was going to help Yano, she'd better suck it up and take her punishment.

Likewise, while I was worried about her, I didn't speak to her any more than usual. I didn't know to what extent our classmates intended to make an example out of Iguchi, so it was best to avoid sticking up for her. Really, there was nothing I could do.

Once our fifth and sixth hours of class were over, we were back in the homeroom, ready to leave for the day. Other than Yano being ignored and harassed, and Iguchi being depressed, it had been a fairly uneventful day. School wrapped up with announcements for next week and our homeroom teacher's usual reminder that "Exams are coming soon!"

Tomorrow was a free day. The thought lightened my spirits, just a little.

After we said our salutations, those who had club activities and those who had arrangements to hang out after school quickly exited the classroom.

Usually, after school, a few students still loitered around the room, gossiping or furtively eating snacks. Today, though, even Kasai and his crew ended up moving to the cafeteria. One by one, the others left as well.

Suddenly, Iguchi and I, the two on duty for the day, were left alone.

Even the girls who were normally friendly with Iguchi had made a swift retreat for fear of getting caught up in whatever was going on—a wise decision. Even I thought it was best to withdraw as much as possible. There was no place for kindness here.

We dutifully went about our tasks, but somehow remaining silent was making things even weirder, so I decided to pass the time with some completely frivolous conversation.

"I heard there's been a kaiju around," I said.

I'm not sure whether the look of shock on her face was due to the fact I'd started talking about something as ridiculous as a kaiju or because I had spoken to her at all. Though she said nothing, she continued looking my way, so I averted my eyes and continued.

"Or at least that's what a lot of people have been saying lately. Story goes that if you look outside at night, you'll see a huge black kaiju walking around. But if you try to take a picture of it, apparently nothing shows up."

I thought that, at the very least, she would give me some kind of reaction. However, she still said nothing, and so I ended up glancing her way. I instantly regretted it.

She was smiling, painfully.

"Th...thank you."

Unlike the stilted way that Yano normally spoke, it sounded as though the words were stopped up inside Iguchi's throat.

I had no idea why she was thanking me. "For what?"

"For trying to make me feel better with that joke. I wasn't expecting that. I know you, Adachi-kun. It isn't like you to try to cheer someone up. And you'd never talk about something as childish as a kaiju."

She chuckled, her voice still seeming a bit pained. I cursed myself.

The only reason that I had even accepted the ridiculous premise of a kaiju running around was because I was the genuine article. It was just one of the stupid things we boys discussed amongst ourselves, things we said without even believing. It was obvious that Iguchi, who knew nothing of the rumors, would take it that way. Especially if I talked about it at a time like this.

Iguchi continued to smile and then spoke to me in a trembling voice. "You saw it, didn't you?"

My heart raced, just as it had that morning. "Don't even worry about it," I replied.

Utterly pointless advice. If everyone could simply go around not worrying about things at will, the world would sure be a carefree place. Real life was harder than that.

"I think it'll be over soon," I said, feeling compelled to keep talking. I feared the silence and that Iguchi might break it by spilling her guts. I couldn't bear the thought of either.

"Yeah. I guess that's just how it goes," she said.

I'm sure that was what everyone in our class thought regarding Iguchi's dejected mood. It surprised me that Iguchi felt the same way. Just how it goes, just how it goes. That was just how things went if you happened to pick up Yano's eraser for her, accident or no. Just how it goes when you put a damper on our class's shared sense of unity. The haranguing, the graffiti. Those were just par for the course.

No matter how many unfortunate incidents piled up, that was just how it was. It wasn't worth worrying about; it was something you tried to not even see. I should have been brushing the whole thing off too, but no one could possibly deny that it was tragic to see Iguchi trying to convince herself of the same thing regarding her circumstance.

It was, and yet my own personal empathy for her was completely off the mark.

"I can't complain, I mean, I..."

She took a longer, deeper breath than usual.

"...I did the same thing to Yano-san."

"You mean ignoring her?"

Iguchi shook her head.

Then she told me about what had happened yesterday after school, after the rest of us had left. She had been interrogated, insulted, her integrity questioned, and attacked without so much as a chance to defend herself. And finally, to prove that she didn't consider Yano to be a member of the class, she was told to write terrible things on Yano's notebook. And so she couldn't complain if someone did the same thing to her.

I was at a loss for words.

Iguchi might have assumed that Yano was the one responsible, that she was out for some kind of payback. But...I don't think she believed that. I realized it partway through her confession, something about the way she spoke to me. It was like she was apologizing to me in place of Yano, in a way that she never could to Yano herself. Normally, one should never voice such sympathy for Yano, but it was just the two of us here, so I didn't bother to stop her.

That said, I don't think me listening to her story made Iguchi's heart any lighter.

For some reason, the whole time she was talking, I kept thinking to myself that Iguchi might be the one outlier in our class.

Perhaps she felt less cautious at the end of our talk because I was the only one there. Or maybe she had just grown desperate? Either way, she confided in me a doubt which no one in our class should ever dare to speak.

"It's so *weird,* Adachi! Why should everyone always be so awful to Yano-san?"

I checked out on the conversation then and there. I didn't so much as reply. Not even a "Yeah" or an "I guess." I turned all of my attention back onto my classroom chores. I wasn't ignoring her, but what else could I do? That was just how it was.

Things would have turned out better if I had made my decision then.

Friday NIGHT

RECALLING A DREAM from my childhood, of having an adventure in a department store after closing time, I decided to sneak into one at night. To think that having a form like this could literally make my dreams come true.

Knowing that no image of me would appear on film, I walked brazenly into the darkened store. Of course, I still had to scale myself down to canine size. I couldn't risk scaring the life out of some poor nightguard.

I warily surveyed the shop's interior from above, standing at the top of the stairs. I couldn't help but notice how eerie the purple glow of the emergency lights was. I didn't think it was unusual to be a bit creeped out, but really, there was barely any difference between the shop now and the shop during the daytime. The theme park had still had employees around to finish work that could probably only be done at night, but the department store had no need for a graveyard shift. Besides a stray flashlight beam that passed near the stairs, there was nothing to get worked up over.

I think that dreams might be more beautiful while they're still in our heads. There was no shelter in this store for a monster like me. But where to go next? If I really put some effort into it, I could probably run all the way to a neighboring land. I could challenge myself to visit every part of our country, gradually expanding my territory.

I proceeded through that nerve-racking space, a tense atmosphere where both time and light seemed to have stopped. Myriad scenes floated through my head.

I had probably made it down to the second or third floor by now. There, I happened upon a corner stand with various goods lined up around it and stopped on the spot.

Perhaps it was because it was a rainy day, or perhaps because the rainy season had arrived, or maybe they were just always there. Whatever the reason, the heaps of colorful girls' umbrellas shined brilliantly to my night-sharp eyes.

Honestly, I was a bit bewildered by the thought that had popped into my head when I saw them. Given that fact, I doubt I made my next decision out of goodwill. I think I just had an opportunity and followed an impulse.

I decided to act. I rushed up to the rooftop, bounded across the roofs of other buildings, and took a brief detour back to my own home. Naturally, I knew my house well and moved through it with all the silence of the night.

I snatched an umbrella from our stand with my tail and climbed to the second floor, opened a window, and leapt back outside. I needed to avoid being seen exiting my house, just in case, so I flew out at my highest speed. Once I confirmed the place I landed was empty, I expanded my size. I couldn't be captured on film, after all. Might as well be a kaiju through and through.

It was surprisingly thrilling to act as though I were a kaiju. Iguchi had gotten it right—there were some unexpectedly childish parts of me. Of course, was it really all that unexpected?

Even running through the rain, I reached the school quickly on my six massive feet. I stretched myself up high, shrank my body down, and landed atop the roof.

From there I had to put a spin on my usual method of entry, as I had not only myself, but the umbrella to sneak inside. This time I would have to actually bother with opening the roof door.

If Yano-san wasn't there, then she wasn't there, and that would be that, I thought. It was raining. I couldn't imagine her coming even on a day like this.

I'm not sure if I was relieved or disappointed to find that I could pull the front door of the classroom open with my tail. Perhaps it was both.

"Even on a night like this, huh?" I said.

As I spoke, Yano-san raised her head. She'd been sitting at her desk, fidgeting with her phone.

"I didn't...think you'd...come."

I closed the door with my tail, moved to the back of the classroom, and changed my size to one more comfortable for sitting.

"You said you'd lost your umbrella. I had an extra one, so here."

"Wah!"

Yano-san let out a puzzled cry when I gently tossed the umbrella her way—it smacked her right in the face.

"Oww. Hey, no...talking about the day...time."

Again with that warning. I dismissed the advice with a "Hmph," wondering just which of us was being the more annoying one here.

She stoically bowed her head. "Still...thank you."

I'd half expected see her usual grin at a time like this, but I wasn't one to go around forcing people to make the expressions I wanted, so I said nothing.

I recalled Iguchi-san and the pained smile upon her face.

Unlike our usual routine, there was something that I actually wanted to discuss with Yano-san today. But how to broach the topic? During the daytime, with someone like Kudou, this would have been a breeze—but I had no idea how to direct a conversation the way that I wanted when it came to Yano-san.

How to open the conversation? As I searched the ceiling of the classroom for an answer, Yano-san again asked a strange question, as though she had suddenly thought of something.

"Acchi...kun, are you...a *Laputa* fan? Or...*Naussica* fan?"

I hesitated, as I was unsure if I should tell the truth or give the prepared answer that I always gave when asked about my favorite Ghibli film.

"Uh, I prefer *Totoro*."

"It was...all just a...dream, but...it wasn't a dream."

A famous line from the movie. For a moment it sounded like a completely different quote, thanks to Yano-san's strange speech pattern.

In that moment, I thought that quote might encapsulate just how being a monster felt to me.

"What about you, Yano-san? *Laputa* or *Naussica?*"

"Ac...tually, I like...*Princess Monono...ke.*"

"Then why did you give me those two other choices?"

Maybe it was because of her fondness for *Princess Mononoke* that she wasn't afraid of seeing me like this at first meeting.

"Actually, Yano-san, shouldn't *your* favorite be *Totoro?*"

"Why...?"

"Well, I mean, your name is Satsuki."

I had only said it as a bit of friendly ribbing, but for some reason she looked a bit peeved—which is to say, she very intentionally wrinkled her brow and pursed her lips, which wasn't in the slightest bit intimidating.

"I'm not...*that* Satsuki."

"No?"

"Though our names...do share the...same meaning: May."

As I tilted that great head of mine, so massive I could swallow Yano-san up in a single gulp, she smugly answered a question I hadn't even asked.

"It's the name of a...flower." Not waiting for my acknowledgment, she continued, "They should be bloo...ming right a...bout now. It's...a little late for...them, but it's a...spring flower."

The phrase "spring flower" conjured up images in my mind of pearly pink sunsets swallowing up the sky and fields of golden blossoms. I had no mental imagery for the flower that shared her name.

"It's...my favorite spring flower. It...would be even if it weren't... my...name."

"Not cherry blossoms, or rapeseed flowers?"

As I tried to convey the image that *Satsuki* gave me, Yano-san nodded. "Of course I...like those...too. But...if I had...to choose, I'd...say I pre...fer flowers that...bloom quietly on a mountain... top or on a back road over the...pretty, showy ones that every... one else loves."

Projecting, much? I thought, unfairly.

Flowers that bloomed quietly, secretly.

A variety of people popped to mind.

"Oh, hey, when...the rain stops, let's go...see some...satsuki. They're blooming in the...mountains."

So far, out of all the plans that Yano-san had proposed, that had to be the best one by far. However...

"I can manage that, but how will *you* get there?" I asked.

"Let me...ride on your...back."

"No way. What happens if you turn into a monster, too?"

I expected her to say something like, *Maybe that wouldn't be so bad.* But instead she immediately abandoned the idea. "That... would suck." I was the one that had brought up the concern, but it still hurt a bit being rejected like that.

"By the way, why'd you start talking about Ghibli all of a sudden?"

"*Naussica* was on...*Kinyou Roadshow.* You didn't...see it?"

"Oh, I forgot. That was today, huh?"

Ghibli films rarely came up in conversation with Kasai and the others, so I hadn't been paying attention. I was a little disappointed—I'd seen the film plenty of times, but I would have liked to watch it again.

"Also, I...was reading this...blog about the behind the...scenes production and urban leg...ends about Ghibli...films."

"Ah, stuff like, 'Is Totoro really a Shinigami?'"

"Yeah, yeah. Acchi...kun, you like shini...gami, huh?"

"I'm pretty sure that rumor's fake."

"Legends...are fun because they're...legends, so it doesn't matter if it's...fake or not. It doesn't...matter, as long as...you like Totoro."

It was annoying to be talked down to, especially by her of all people. All I had said was that I heard the rumor was false. I hadn't insisted on it or tried to force my opinion on her, and yet she criticized me for it all the same. However, I didn't debate her on it, since I happened to agree: legends were fun because they were legends. They were tales meant to be spread far and wide, not overanalyzed and picked apart.

I worked up my courage and decided to try and broach the topic I'd wanted to discuss with her.

"Iguchi-san said almost the same thing."

"Igu...chan did?"

This little "Igu...chan" phrase that Yano-san had been saying since yesterday was strangely intoned, perhaps something that she had never actually called our classmate in person. Regardless, she had taken the bait.

"Yeah, Iguchi-san used to sit next to me last year. She always had a Totoro key chain on her bag, so I asked her about it one time, about whether she really liked Totoro. We talked a lot about it, and she said the same thing. She said that she loved things that are mysterious, especially while they're still shrouded in mystery. After I heard that, I went and watched *Totoro* again with that in mind, and it became my favorite, too."

"...Huh?"

Yano-san seemed bewildered.

"I mean, uh..."

Crap. I'd let myself get worked up and started babbling about my own interests when I should have just gotten straight to the point. I'm sure that she didn't want to hear about all that, and I hadn't intended to say it.

As I stood there, embarrassed, I realized that she hadn't chided me for talking about things from during the day. I suppose memories have nothing to do with either noon or night.

"Uh, anyway, the reason I mentioned Iguchi-san is that I wanted you to know that she was the one who wrote all over your notebook, but she didn't want to do it. Other people forced her. I learned about that today, and Iguchi-san felt bad, and she was sorry for it. I thought that you should know."

Hoping that it would alleviate some of my embarrassment, I rushed headlong into what I had originally wanted to say. Of course, after I said it, I realized I had no idea what I would do if Yano-san suddenly filled with rage towards Iguchi-san. No matter how apologetic Iguchi-san was, no matter how much she regretted it, she had still done it, after all. Such a reaction wouldn't be strange at all.

For a moment, there was silence. Just how was she going to react? What would she say? As I stood there fretting, Yano-san, with a dumbfounded look still on her face, said simply, softly, "I see."

She saw what? As I waited, she pointed at me with her little finger.

"Acchi...kun, you..."

And then, a smile spread across her face, like a little flower in full bloom.

"...you *like* Igu-chan...don't you?"

A puff of air that sounded very much like "Wha?" spilled from my jagged mouth, and Yano-san gave a theatrical nod of understanding.

"I see...I see. You...should talk a bit more carefully about the girl...you like, though."

"Huh? Wait a...hold on, what?"

My panic was incredibly obvious. As always, Yano-san entirely ignored my response and patted her fist onto her palm. Hang on now. My emotions couldn't keep up with this.

"I see...why it was a notebook I...already used up. Because it was...Igu...chan."

"What do you mean?"

"Daytime talk is...over now."

Yano-san clasped both hands over her mouth. Well, that was sudden.

Just where did she draw the line? It was starting to feel like this whole thing was at the mercy of her whims, so I decided to ignore her advice. There was something that I desperately could not keep silent about.

"So, by the way..."

There was one more thing that I wanted to confirm, just in case. I needed to talk about this seriously, for the sake of calming my own nerves.

"About the graffiti on Iguchi-san's notebook..."

Her mouth still covered, Yano-san furrowed her eyebrows.

"I just have to be sure. It wasn't you, right?"

This time, with her mouth still covered, and her eyebrows still furrowed, she shook her head. "Of course not. Sorry."

Though I'd meant that I was sorry for doubting her, Yano-san pointed my way, as if to lecture me.

"It's...mid...night...break."

Apparently, that edict was far more important to her than the fact of my suspicion.

There was a violent sound against the window. The downpour seemed to be growing stronger.

Just then, the bell rang. Between my trip to the department store, and the fact that I had transformed later in the evening than usual, tonight's visit was a short one.

"Time to...go. Acchi...kun, I'm glad that Igu...chan is the one... who's important to...you."

"Hey. No talking about the daytime."

I realized that by saying that, I acknowledged her decree, but not even a monster has the power to take back words that have already flown from its mouth.

"It makes the night...less...important, you know?" Her words were teasing but pure. I was at a loss for a reply.

So I said nothing. No "yeah," no "uh-huh." No matter what I said, I couldn't help but feel that I would be the one who ended up getting hurt.

"I hate seeing...good people...get hurt," she said in parting, just before I leapt from the window. Even at this, I couldn't shake my shaggy black head.

It was not something I could deny.

Without saying another word, I leapt outside. The rain battered my body, but it made no difference to a monster like me.

I wonder. If I had simply said "yeah," would that have changed anything?

If I had said "uh-huh," would that have changed anything?

The next week, something dreadful happened.

At Night,
I Become a Monster

Monday
DAY

I HAVE TO CONFESS, I did stop back in at the school on Saturday night as well, but Yano wasn't there. It seemed there was no such thing as midnight break on the weekend.

The rain had let up on Sunday, but on Monday the sky was still shrouded in grey clouds.

My number one concern on this day was not whether I could keep myself from slipping up or whether I could avoid having any one-on-one exchanges with Yano. It was whether or not Iguchi was going to show up at school.

Honestly, it was weird that Yano was able to proudly come to school, day in and day out, despite how she was treated. No one could blame Iguchi if she never showed up at the classroom again—nor Yano, for that matter.

Still, it would definitely be better for Iguchi if she came. If she took the day off, everyone would know that what happened on Thursday was the reason. Might as well get it over with—the more time went by, the harder it would be to keep from coming back to school. Also, we had exams coming up this year, so it was best to show up every day.

Of course, that was merely my public stance on the matter. Internally, I couldn't help but worry that Iguchi had been so hurt by my ignoring her last comment that she wouldn't be able to show up at all. I felt a huge weight lift off my chest when I entered the classroom and saw Iguchi sitting at her desk— even if I couldn't ignore the fact that no one else was standing around her.

"Weather's got even you down, huh?" Kasai spoke up as I arrived at my seat, sitting himself down atop my desk without so much as a greeting. "Looks like no soccer today, I guess."

I quickly rearranged my face. "Yeah, guess not."

"Hey, sour face, I got somethin' exciting for ya."

Whenever Kasai said he had something "exciting" to tell me, it was usually some factoid that he'd heard on TV, or gossip about our classmates' love affairs, or something even more trivial. What could he possibly have to say this time?

"Something happen?"

"Yeah, yeah! You remember what I was sayin' about that kaiju, right?"

"Right, the one that comes out at night."

"Apparently, it's been spotted near the school."

"What?" I replied, decently surprised. Of course, I should have realized that at that size, someone could probably spot me from far away. But it turned out that was not the case.

"So like, apparently Motoda snuck into the school on Friday night."

"...What?"

Without meaning to, I let out an unadulterated, genuine reaction.

"Ahaha! I've seen that look before." Kasai laughed guilelessly, clapping his hands. "He's such an idiot. Apparently, he realized in the middle of the night that he forgot his mitt in the club room. He had a game first thing in the morning, and he was worried that his coach was gonna kill him, so he came here. He's definitely got a bike at home, but like, it was raining, hah. But apparently when he got here, the gate was open, and he just walked right in. Luckily the lock on the club room's broken, so he got in and got the mitt. It was just when he was leaving that it showed up."

As I grew more nervous, Kasai slapped my shoulder.

"The kaiju?"

"Yeah, apparently it's crazy huge when you see it up close and super creepy. He called me in the middle of the night, all worked up. He really needed to tell someone. Right, you'd have been asleep then."

I gave a modest "sorry" in response to the jab.

"Anyway, he was hiding in the shadows of the clubroom watching this thing, then it jumped up high all of a sudden, and when it came down it got smaller and vanished into the school."

"The hell?"

"Right? When I asked if he expected me to believe that, he got all huffy and said that when he came to the school again on Saturday, it showed up again. Honestly, I think he was just dreaming, but apparently that idiot actually snuck *inside* the school building. He's so stupid."

"Seriously?"

"Yeah, now he wants to try and sneak a bunch of guys into the school to try and catch the kaiju. Ahaha, I honestly can't wait for them to all get caught by the guards."

"Ahah...hahaha... Good point."

Though I forced a laugh, my heart quivered inside my chest.

This was bad, I thought. But then, when I considered it again, I realized that really, there was nothing bad about it at all.

As long as I never came near the school again, I'd be fine. That way, Motoda and his crew would realize that no monster was going to show up at the school, and I'd be somewhere far away where none of my classmates could see me. My nights would be peaceful as they had always been.

Yes, *my* peaceful night was assured. But Yano on the other hand? Her solitude was going to be destroyed.

Just as Kasai had said, the best outcome would be for Motoda and the others to be caught by the guards. It wouldn't be good for them, of course, but it would be a huge help for Yano. However, if Motoda and his crew managed to sneak into the school undetected, as Yano did, and they ran into her there, things would be very bad.

Or worse—what if they were to encounter her when she was on her *way* to the school...?

No matter who came across me when I was a monster, no matter where, I could simply make myself larger and escape, and they could never catch me. But what could Yano do? The quiet peace of a young girl, without any powers to change her size or run like the wind, would disappear.

The midnight breaks that Yano spoke of would be ruined. What could I do?

I probably *had* to do something, even if, honestly, this was none of my business at all.

I pulled at my hair as Kasai went to spread the tale around to the other factions of our class, only coming back to my senses when Takao let out a loud "I can't believe this!"

Initially, I assumed he was responding to the story about Motoda, but something about his reaction seemed a bit different.

I found out that Takao had ridden his bike here in the morning on Friday but left it at the school because it was raining so hard, having gotten a ride home from his parents instead. But apparently someone had stolen his bike over the weekend.

If it disappeared on Saturday, the thief was probably someone from one of the sports clubs. However, saying something like that in a class with a fair number of members in said clubs would make things awkward, which was probably why he had elected to shout and let everyone know at once—both out of a conscientious effort not to ruin our class's sense of unity and out of fear of making enemies.

I remembered a time in our second year when Yano made a fuss about someone having stolen her pencil box only for it to turn out that she had forgotten it at home.

"Acchi, Acchi!"

"Hm?"

There came a sudden shout from beside me—Kudou. As I turned to look at her, I realized that there was some sort of liquid dripping onto my pants.

"Ah!"

A nosebleed. I quickly dug through my pockets, but I hadn't brought a tissue or handkerchief.

"I'll go get a tissue from Noto," I said, hurrying from the room with my hand pressed to my mouth. I didn't want to cause any bother to the people sitting around me. I heard a loud laugh come from behind me. Kasai was probably telling some funny story. My heart was pounding fast, but I ignored it as always. Why would I get a nosebleed all of a sudden? Were the consequences of turning into a monster finally catching up with me?

I pushed the door to the nurse's office open with my non-bloodied hand, tasting iron in my mouth. Inside, I saw Noto and an unexpected guest. It was Midorikawa.

"Knock first, Adachi," Noto admonished me.

"Could I have a tissue?"

As I made my terse request, offering neither apology nor greeting, Noto handed me a tissue box. I took several out, wiped my hand and mouth, and stopped up my nose.

"Take this, too," she instructed.

I took the offered wet wipe and peered into a small mirror on the wall, cleaning up my face. In the corner of the reflection, I saw Midorikawa looking at me.

"Thank you so much," I said. "And sorry for not knocking."

"Boys aren't the only ones who come here, you know. You have to be more careful."

"I'm sorry. Apologies, Midorikawa," I said.

"Mm," she replied.

Just as I gripped the doorknob, with an "I'll be off, then" sort of wave and started to leave, Noto asked me, "How did you get that nosebleed?" A fair question.

"It just started all of a sudden. I wasn't even doing anything," I told her.

"I see. I said so before, but don't push yourself too hard. If you ever need it, come here and rest."

I said nothing. Just what was it she knew that would make her say that?

She knew nothing about me, or our class, or Yano, and yet she was telling me not to push myself. It was utterly useless advice, just as much as me telling Iguchi "not to worry about it" that past Friday.

Could it be that Midorikawa had been telling Noto about what was going on in our class? I wondered, but it was weird enough for my classmate to be talking at all. Surely no teacher would simply let things go if they knew of our class's situation—even though, logically, there must have been teachers who suspected.

"If you'll excuse me," I said.

This time I successfully left the room, though I did wonder why Midorikawa was there. Was something wrong with her physically? Or was she just doing as Noto had suggested and taking a break after pushing herself too hard? Whichever it was,

I presumed, she seemed like a fragile person and was probably easily damaged, both mentally and physically.

I suddenly wondered: What about Midorikawa?

How did *she* feel about Yano's bullying? At first, she might have thought that it served her right, angry that Yano had destroyed something so important to her. But how did she feel now? She couldn't possibly still be angry at this point, after so many months had passed.

Of course...if she didn't feel that anymore, then what *would* she feel?

I couldn't dwell on things like that. Nor should I have felt obligated to do something about what might happen with Motoda and Yano at night. Nor should I have been concerning myself with Iguchi. At this rate, I would be ostracized by the class, too. I couldn't let that happen.

On the staircase along the way to the classroom, I spotted Yano ahead of me, climbing the stairs, her small body swaying. I swerved past her as quickly as I could. I heard a "Good...morning," from behind, but I successfully ignored it. It would be fine. I was fine.

As I calmed down and returned to the classroom, I was greeted by laughter from Kasai.

"Thinking dirty thoughts, huh?" he asked.

"I was not," I replied, returning to my seat after the light-hearted exchange.

Kudou, who had been the first to notice my nosebleed, gave me a worried look. "What happened?"

"It was nothing."

Everything was fine. I was just like everyone else. Just when I was about to offer some kind of situationally appropriate reply, like, "Guess I shouldn't have been eating chocolate first thing in the morning," Yano entered the room.

"Good...morning."

Her greeting went ignored. Yano was smiling that self-satisfied smile, as always.

Normally, Yano would notice some change in one of our classmates and try to strike up a one-sided conversation about it and then head for her seat as someone clicked their tongue at her.

Normally.

Today was different.

This time, Yano strode up to Iguchi.

Her manner reminded me of an incident that had happened one day a while back, when the communal dynamic of our class had shifted, just a little. Well, no, it hadn't changed; it was always the way it was now, I was just late to realize it.

It was something about the way she walked that reminded me of that day.

Just as Midorikawa had back then, Iguchi raised her head silently, staring at Yano, who was standing right before her. Perhaps she was thinking, *What does she want?* Or maybe it was, *Don't mess with me.* I was sitting behind Iguchi, so all I could see was the queasy expression on Yano's face.

The scene unfolded in the edges of my vision. After giving me a wink, Kudou turned to focus on the pair, as though she had just then noticed what was going on.

I barely had time to wonder what Yano was planning, except perhaps to realize that Iguchi's face was angled the exact perfect degree to match up with short little Yano.

Yano suddenly slapped her across the face.

The sound of the slap—the unimaginable sound of one girl striking another—the "Eek!" that came from Iguchi just before it, the sound of someone standing up just after, and the "Hey!" that slipped unbidden from my mouth—all of them seemed to ring out at once.

Chaos erupted.

Yano cried out in pain as Nakagawa, one of the girls who had previously been shunning Iguchi, grabbed Yano by the hair. She tried to stop Yano from seizing Iguchi's bag, demanding to know what she was doing. Despite that, Yano smacked the bag feebly into Iguchi, as Motoda, just back from morning practice, asked curiously what was going on. The homeroom teacher stormed in, and his angry shout echoed over the sound of the ringing bell. Everyone was pulled aside and questioned, but Yano refused to answer. Instead, the other girls around explained that Yano had attacked Iguchi without warning—which was true. No one else offered any differing testimony, and Yano had no excuse to give. On the contrary, she was smiling—smugly, as always.

I saw that look, and a chill ran down my spine.

As the teacher took Yano by the hand and exited the room, the classroom—though we had been ordered to remain silent— erupted in a cacophony.

"The hell is with her?!"

"You see that?!"

"Igu-chan, you okay?"

"I'm gonna kill her!"

Amidst the din sat Iguchi, looking around herself and timidly taking in the room.

I was equally frenzied. What had just happened?

Though of course no one but Yano herself would know the truth, our classmates began to formulate some theories about what had fueled her behavior.

The most popular girls in the class confessed that Iguchi had been the one to vandalize Yano's notebook but also that they had been involved themselves. Perhaps, they speculated, it had been the straw that broke the camel's back, and Yano had decided to enact revenge on sweet and gentle Iguchi, something that she would normally be unable to do.

I doubt that I could have said anything if I had any alternative theories to offer, but the fact was that I didn't. In fact, I felt responsible. I'd been the one who informed Yano of Iguchi's involvement the night before. No matter how guilty she may have felt, Iguchi should have apologized to Yano herself, so one could not expect Yano's anger to clear up as simply as that. Perhaps she had taken such out-of-character revenge this time, despite saying that she wouldn't, simply because it was Iguchi.

Iguchi was a nice girl.

Why had I taken Yano's words at face value when she said them? It was *Yano*, after all. And yet I had wholeheartedly accepted what she'd said.

The class was indignant.

"It's ridiculous to get violent towards Igu-chan just for writing on her stuff," said Kudou.

"Y-yeah, seriously," I replied, hesitantly nodding. I couldn't pinpoint exactly why I thought Kudou's statement didn't quite hit the mark, when I thought about it after.

Just like Kudou, the general sentiment in the rest of our class was that Yano's little act of revenge was way out of line—and violence totally over the top. I could agree with that much. But it was hard to accept the group assertion that defacing or destroying someone's belongings was somehow a lesser sin than violence.

Would she have escaped similar denouncement if she had merely ripped up Iguchi's beloved Totoro key chain? Obviously not—it was for the crime of destroying a beloved item that she faced this bullying in the first place.

I happened to look at Iguchi's bag then, hanging from her desk. *Huh?* I thought. The little Totoro, who was always so steadfastly fastened to her bag, was missing.

Just then, a single silhouette entered through the door at the front of the classroom. It was not our homeroom teacher, nor Yano, but Noto instead.

"Now then, class, it's time for greetings."

A murmur spread throughout the room at the customary signal, which Noto gave without skipping a beat. Apparently, she was to be our substitute for the day.

"Well, look who's here," Kasai teased, receiving a chilling glare in return.

Though the class didn't truly settle down, we managed to move through our daily greetings, after which Noto opened her notepad and gave the morning announcements. For the first time, it occurred to me that the school nurse would participate in the morning faculty meeting as well. After a brief rundown of the administrative notes, she said: "Now, please keep it down until first period begins. Iguchi-san, would you come with me a moment?" Just like that, she led Iguchi away.

A strange atmosphere, even quieter than before, fell over the classroom, the sort of tense air that could only serve to increase one's frustrations.

For one thing, the fact that no one was worried about Yano's long-standing mistreatment being reported to the homeroom teacher only made the atmosphere feel more tense and weird.

But what did we have to worry about? Even if Yano were to speak the truth, the rest of the class merely had to vehemently rebuke her, making it altogether a sort of moral lesson, and that would be the end of that. On top of that, no direct violence had ever been done to her, so she had no proof. Surely everyone knew as much.

There was no point in criticizing or getting angry with anyone if they refused to believe that they were in the wrong.

Things can only get worse for you when you're in the wrong. The bullying can grow more insidious, less conspicuous. The most dangerous enemy is an unseen one.

Our first period on Mondays was an extended homeroom. About two minutes after the bell, our teacher returned with a self-satisfied Yano and a bewildered-looking Iguchi in tow.

The lesson plan for first period was devoted entirely to calming down the unsettled class. Our teacher explained that what happened this morning was a conflict strictly between the two girls, they'd already apologized to each other, and though the problem that arose was one merely between them, we should please remember that we were all comrades on the road to graduation and not let this affect your exam preparations, and various other platitudes.

The remainder of the period was devoted to self-directed study. The time was meant to be occupied by lesson prep and completing homework that we had forgotten to bring, but the room was awash with whispers, as though no one at all was concentrating on this task. Midorikawa passed the time reading a book.

Anyone could probably guess what happened after that. When the period ended, a crowd gathered around Iguchi. Everyone expressed their worries and sympathies, and the other girls offered overexaggerated apologies.

No one bothered to approach Yano and ask "What's your problem?!" or anything like that. She merely had her desk kicked away at break time, was struck with countless spitballs during lessons, and had her shoes soaked with water at the end of cleanup.

And yet the strange, addled Yano grinned throughout it all.

As I watched her on the way home, pitching forward as someone stomped on her heel, I again realized how little I understood her.

Monday
NIGHT

WHEN I STEPPED OUTSIDE, I spied the moon peeking out from the clouds. I ran beneath the moonlight. I was not thrilled with the task ahead of me, but I knew that I needed to say something. Maybe I felt some twisted sense of obligation, since I was probably the only one who could get some honest answers about this.

In short, I was headed for the school.

"What was that all about?" was the first thing I said to Yano-san upon entering the classroom. She was sitting at her desk, apparently playing a game on her phone, before she looked up at me. "Oh...you came."

"This morning. What was that?" I continued, moving towards the more spacious rear of the classroom and shifting my body to my usual size.

"This...morning?"

"With Iguchi."

When I tried to press her, she gave her typical, tiresome reply.
"No talking...about the daytime."

"You do not get to pull that right now."

"You're so...annoying, Acchi...kun."

"I could say the same about you."

"It's not like...you did anything...about it."

She had a point. Now that she mentioned it, I hadn't. When I mulled it over again, wondering just why I felt so viscerally moved by this, I soon realized.

"So what happened to not wanting to hurt nice people?" I asked.

"I don't...*want* to."

"So then why?" I demanded again.

Yano-san pursed her lips. The look on her face resembled the faces of adults I remembered seeing as a small child, as though she were looking annoyedly at a toddler making some selfish demand. She heaved a theatrical sigh and opened those pursed lips to speak.

"No one's... ignoring Igu-chan anymore...are they?"

With an air that strongly suggested that she had been forced to say something that she did not want to, Yano-san once again returned to her game.

Though I had been the one to raise the question, I hadn't prepared myself for the reply. I felt eviscerated by her words. It felt as though the earth had just moved beneath my feet, though it hadn't.

"Daytime talk...is over now."

"Wha?"

"It's cloudy...but the rain stopped. Let's...do something."

With a sound effect that sounded very much like a Game Over, Yano-san slipped her phone back into her pocket and looked out the window. I followed her gaze and was startled to see something moving in the building across the field. But when I looked closely, I realized it was just the shifting moonlight playing tricks on my eyes.

I was still flustered by Yano-san's words, by the reason for her actions.

Still, it was a bit strange.

"Iguchi-san was the one who wrote on your notebook, though."

"So I heard. You keep...saying...the same things."

"That's because you keep ignoring them."

I couldn't understand her. Iguchi-san was most certainly a nice girl. However, that was only as far as I, living on the inside of our class's united front, was concerned. Iguchi-san had actively ignored Yano-san for months, and Yano-san had to have known how shaken Iguchi-san was in the moment that she'd picked up that eraser. She would never had picked it up if she hadn't been caught off guard.

So, was Yano-san really saying that she made herself a scapegoat for the sake of even *that* amount of kindness?

"I don't understand you."

"You keep...repeating yourself, Acchi-kun. Did you forget... what you said yourself?"

"What do you mean?"

"That mysteries...are only mysteries...when they're mysterious."

"Iguchi-san was the one who said that."

The black droplets across my body trembled but not out of irritation or malice. This was an uneasy feeling that my heart did not know how to handle, like the sensation of seeing a shape or a color I had never seen before.

"S-so you're fine with that?"

"With...what?" she asked.

"I mean..."

With the fact that things were going to become even worse for her than they ever were before, I wanted to say, but could not find the words to do so.

I don't know what Yano-san thought in response to my wordless hesitation, but she grinned smugly. "Well...I don't know."

Did she mean that she didn't understand my question? Or did she mean that even she wasn't sure that she'd done the right thing? The former would be best, as the latter would mean that she really was an odd duck, someone who couldn't ever follow the flow of a conversation or read the room.

Of course, when I imagined the ramifications of that, I grew afraid.

So far, I had lived under the assumption that Yano-san was a girl who operated by a sort of logic that the rest of us could never grasp; a girl who seemed to live every day to its fullest, who always wore a grin on her face even when she was ignored or shunned or bullied. A girl who suddenly attacked classmates during morning homeroom.

A twisted, addled girl.

With someone like that, one might be able to think that the sort of treatment she received was inevitable.

But what did it mean if she was just someone who was working and living the best way she knew how, by her own philosophy? What did it mean if, after spending the whole weekend agonizing over it, Yano-san had decided to come to the rescue of a classmate who had become embroiled in something heinous thanks to a momentary interaction with her?

I suddenly began to worry that there had been some similar situation with Midorikawa-san, that Yano-san had done what she did out of following her own Yano-san line of reasoning. But I didn't ask about it. If I asked, and was met with some rationale that I had no choice but to accept, then I would no longer be able to hide behind our class's sense of righteousness.

I shook my head and forcefully banished the thought from my mind. That just couldn't be. There was no way that a normal person could carry on with such a smug look on their face, day in and day out, while dealing with Yano-san's burdens. No normal person would make their already poor circumstance worse just to help a classmate who didn't even like them. Even then, there had to be far more normal ways to help than a slap in the face.

There was no doubt about it. This girl lived by a mindset that was thoroughly different from the rest of ours. That much was certain.

The fact that she liked the same music I did, that she was a fellow *Jump* reader, and that she also looked forward to *Kinyou Roadshow* was totally irrelevant.

I decided to stop talking about Iguchi-san. No matter how much we discussed the topic, there was nothing that I could do to change the circumstances, so it was pointless.

Instead, I decided to discuss an issue that I might *actually* be able to understand. That would be far more constructive.

"Th-that reminds me, there was something else that I came here to talk to you about, Yano-san."

Yano-san looked at me suspiciously. "Only if it's not something about...the daytime...again."

"It's not. Or, I don't think it is. Truth is, one of the guys from our class saw me coming to the school, so he was apparently saying he's gonna sneak in here to catch me."

"Wow...how stupid."

"Seriously. Catching a monster?"

"No, I meant...you...Acchi-kun."

When I shot a stern glare at her with all eight of my eyes, Yano-san chuckled. Now that she was accustomed to them, it must have looked a bit more comical than it would have coming from a more human stare.

"That's...no good."

"Right? Also, he seems to have figured out how easy it is to sneak into here."

"Then he knows about...midnight break."

"I don't know about that, but even if we avoid coming here until those guys get bored of hunting a kaiju, what if this place ends up becoming a long-term hangout for them? Even laying low wouldn't fix the problem."

"What if...you scared them away...at the gates?"

"That would be fine if I could come here early and lie in wait for them, but I'm never sure exactly what time I'm going to change into a monster each night."

I tried to direct her away from any plans that relied solely on my effort. This was the nighttime. No one should be seeing me.

Yano-san folded her arms and grumbled. "If they come...at any time outside of midnight break...the guard will catch them, so it should be...fine. And...if they come during midnight break... you'll just have to make sure they never think of sneaking in...ever again."

"I guess so. Scaring them off outside of the school wouldn't stop them from wanting to sneak in, anyway."

Suddenly, a creepy laugh erupted from Yano-san. "Eeheehee-heeheehee!"

"What is it?" I asked.

"No, it's just... I'm so...happy to have you protecting this place...Acchi-kun."

Though I had purposely tried to ignore that fact, hearing it said out loud was a bit embarrassing.

It wasn't like that. It was merely that I, being a monster, might actually have the ability to drive them away.

But another strange thought crossed my mind: that I might somehow be trying to atone for things I had done during the day.

"Well, anyway, if I can get more details about their plans, then you probably shouldn't come here on the day it goes down," I said.

"And just how will you let me know...the timing?"

"I, uh..."

If I only found out on the day they planned to do it, there wouldn't be enough time to get word to her. As I told her before, the time which I turned into a monster every night was not set— and I couldn't talk to her during the daytime.

"And...also..."

"Hm?"

"What would you do? If it was...today?"

As if perfectly timed to Yano-san's words, when I tried to respond to the thought, there came a sound like a large bell ringing from outside the window.

The alarm. My body trembled, oversensitive to the noise. We looked to one another and both immediately crouched down. *We've been spotted,* I thought. The alarm bell was sudden.

My eight eyes darted back and forth wildly as I crept towards the front door alongside Yano-san, when suddenly, the bell stopped. As it did, Yano-san immediately turned to me.

"That seems...strange."

"What does?" I asked, my voice strained.

Yano-san stood. "I figured we might have been spotted by some...teacher...who came here and didn't know about midnight break... Since...the guards shouldn't have a problem with us. But...the alarm only rang...over in the other building. And it... was quiet."

She was clearly flustered. As I thought about it, besides the whole "midnight break" thing, everything she said was correct, so I summoned up a Shadow and sent it flying out into the courtyard.

Naturally, there was no one there. When I snuck into the opposing building and had a thorough look around, there was no one there either. A light was on in the guard room, but there was no indication of anything actually going on. I moved outside, looked out across the fields and then turned towards the gates.

There, through the Shadow's eyes, I caught a glimpse of movement.

It was only for a moment, and there was barely enough time to confirm that it was a human passing through the gates before they vanished out of sight. I hurried to chase after them, but the second I passed through the gates, my connection to the Shadow's sight was severed.

"What's...wrong?" Yano-san asked.

"The Shadow vanished."

"Oh, you call that thing...Shadow? How embarassing."

"Yeah, whatever. Anyway, I saw someone," I told her.

"Who?"

Who indeed. I'd at least seen that they were wearing a jersey, had shorter hair, and were not very tall. Still, it was only for an instant that I saw them. As I described what I'd seen, Yano-san flopped into her chair, grumbling.

"Maybe...it was someone from outside the school...who came because they heard the bell. Maybe the guard or the teacher...or whoever... rang it."

"No, it looked like they were wearing one of our school's jerseys."

"Well, this is midnight break...so if that's true, then they're probably some total idiot who let their own alarm go off...or something," she said wearily, conveniently ignoring her own idiocy in sneaking into the school every night. Hearing the word "idiot," however, it occurred to me that it might have been some-one from Motoda's squad, an individual sent ahead for reconnais-sance. Or worse, there might already be more of them hanging around in the school...

Ever the worrywart, I once more summoned up my Shad...er, my *clone self* and checked out the interiors of both buildings. In the end, however, I found no one but the guards.

"Did Mister Shadow...find anything?"

"...No, nothing."

Honestly, in what world does a monster get teased by a little girl?

There was no way that we were going to be able to get any more information about who I had seen. Instead, Yano-san and I discussed how to deal with Motoda and company. I silently continued my surveillance throughout. Unfortunately, we were unable to come up with any sort of special measures, and in the end, we decided that I would chase them down with a clone if they snuck in during midnight break, menacing them with fire like some sort of wild beast.

Though I said that this was a discussion, it was mostly just me offering up ideas while Yano-san chattered about nonsense in between.

Finding myself at a loss in the midst of it, I confessed: "You know, Yano-san, I'm doing this for you."

To which she peevishly replied, "Well...that's patronizing."

Finally, as always, came the chime that signaled the end of midnight break.

"Time...to go home."

As I lifted up my shrunken body, Yano-san stood as well and then stared hard at me.

"What's up?"

"Will you come again...tomorrow?"

I hadn't heard that question in a while. I started to wonder why it was that she had asked me that again today, but then stopped myself.

"They might show up without warning, so I'll be here. Hide yourself somewhere while I'm not here."

It really would be for the best, I thought, *if she learned to be more cautious.* To Yano-san, there was nothing that caused her more uneasiness than the thought of her midnight break being ruined.

I could not see her face as she waved me away on parting, and my heart filled with worry about what would happen tomorrow.

At Night,
 I Become a Monster

Tuesday
DAY

I THINK I'VE ALREADY alluded to this well enough, but it's
a fundamental truth—whether you're human or monster,
whether you're good or bad, whether it's noon or night, no one
really likes to see bad things happen to others. Thus, I was fully
aware that life at school, starting today, was going to become really
unpleasant. I would have to sit and watch a certain classmate face
even more loathsome treatment than she ever had before. And I
would have to do it without letting anyone see how uncomfort-
able I was with the whole thing.

Realizing this, I steeled myself, but naturally all the resolve
I thought I had mustered to make it through the day was blown
away by reality—a reality that was leagues worse than anything I
could have possibly imagined.

When I arrived at the classroom in the morning, things were
immediately different from usual. For one, Motoda was already

there, which probably wasn't *that* strange; his coach might have had something come up, which would mean no morning practice. What concerned me the most was seeing the girls surrounding a particular desk—Nakagawa's. When I glanced over, half out of politeness's sake, wondering whether something had happened, I saw that Nakagawa was in her seat, crying.

At first, I assumed that she had just broken up with her boyfriend or something. She had a pretty face and a nice body, so she was popular with the boys in our class. And plenty of people worried about getting cheated on. Her tear-soaked face made her seem like a completely different girl from the other day when she had looked at Iguchi like she was a cockroach.

It was when Yano arrived at school that I realized the issue wasn't something merely as simple as that.

She entered the classroom as she did every day, greeting the room with a "Good...morning." Despite yesterday's strange occurrence, as per her custom, she then headed to her seat, no one so much as reacting to her.

Yano was her usual self. What was different was everyone else.

Nakagawa's desk was in the front of the classroom. As Yano started to pass beside them, Motoda, who was also there, smacked her in the back of the head with an empty plastic bottle.

"Hey," he said.

It was a far softer sound than that of yesterday's slap, but it was enough for everyone in the room to freeze in their tracks and look at the pair.

Yano turned to look at him, stunned at both his voice and the unprompted attack. Everyone knew that Motoda had previously done numerous things to Yano, but no one, including him, had ever laid hands on her directly.

Even without knowing the dynamics of our class, it was obvious at a glance which one of them could overpower the other from their difference in size alone.

As the tension in the room rose, everyone wondering what exactly was going to happen, it was Motoda who was the first to speak again.

"It was you, wasn't it?"

I had no idea what he was referring to. Yano cocked her head as though she didn't either.

"I was...what?"

That bizarre speech pattern of Yano's only ever made people angrier.

"You tore up Nakagawa's shoes and threw them out in the yard, didn't you? As payback for yesterday."

Did that really happen? I wondered. From my seat, I glanced at Nakagawa's feet, which is when I finally noticed the brown slippers she was wearing.

"Don't play games with me," Motoda said.

What lingered inside of Motoda, the root of the forceful edge with which he spoke, was not a sense of justice, nor righteous fury on Nakagawa's behalf. It wasn't even disdain—instead, it a pure and simple desire. The desire to harm Yano. I think we all realized it, but such matters were of no consequence to the members of our class.

If I had advice for Yano, then I wish I could have given it to her before. I probably should have done so the previous night. I could have told her the correct facial expression to make when someone says something like that to you. If she had just shaken her head from side to side, given a meek denial with a tense look upon her face, she would have been fine. If she did that, then unless the other person had proof of the accusation, which usually was not the case, then they would calm immediately down.

So *why* would she make *that* face?

"I don't know...anything about that," she said with a grin, flat-out denying the accusation.

"Come again?"

"*III...dooon't knooow...aaanyyything...about that,*" she said again, stretching out each and every word as though he hadn't heard her, before turning and heading toward her seat, that self-satisfied smirk still on her face.

Perhaps she believed that sharing a smile with the world was a surefire technique to make friends with other people. Perhaps in her twisted mind, so long as she always smiled, always laughed, then others would be endeared to her.

If so, then I needed to teach her: no, that's wrong. If you smile at someone who doesn't want to see your smile, then you're only going to rub them the wrong way.

It was because she made that face.

"Wipe that smile off your face," snarled Motoda, taking a rectangular blackboard eraser that was sitting on the ledge of the blackboard in hand. "*You creepy little—!*"

He called her a truly foul name.

And without a moment's hesitation, he flung the eraser at her. Luckily, the side that struck the back of her head was the softer one. As it fell to the floor, the people near her jumped back, as though a dead bug had just come flying their way. It was an object that had come in contact with Yano, after all.

"Wah!" said Yano, pressing her hand to her skull. But as she took her seat, the grin still remained on her face.

Seeing that look, I grew frightened again. How could she smile even at a time like this? Was this just some stubbornness or something on her part?

There were no other overtures made towards Yano that morning. Until the teacher arrived, the whole class was occupied with the matter of the still-crying Nakagawa's shoes, but ultimately, the culprit was never found, and Nakagawa spent the whole day wearing visitor's slippers.

It was our teacher who picked up the eraser, admonishing us, "Who did this? Put things back where they belong."

As I watched, I wondered who could possibly manage to pick it up, when it was too awful for any of us to even say who it had struck.

— ✳ —

The class unanimously decided that Yano was the culprit behind the shoe incident. Naturally, I had no idea what the truth was, and so I could neither confirm nor deny. I merely went along with the flow.

During gym class, standing behind the net that divided the gymnasium's court in two, Nakagawa and the other girls ganged up on Yano. The game of the day was dodgeball, and Yano became the target of relentless, skull-thumping throws, over and over again. But what could I do? There was no point in dwelling on it. Nor on the fact that Iguchi appeared to be watching the other girls with distress. I needed to think about something more useful.

After we finished eating our lunches at midday break, Kasai and I were washing our hands in the restroom while everyone else headed out to the field. I asked him, as though I had only just happened to remember: "Oh yeah, so, is Motoda seriously gonna try to go after that kaiju?"

Motoda himself was in the classroom napping, perhaps to replenish his energy stores for club activities later.

Kasai smiled, amused. "I mean, he said he was, but he's an idiot. There was already that whole thing about him getting into a fight with a first-year on the baseball team, ahaha."

A fight? That was the first I was hearing of it.

"Like, he seemed happy when he said there wasn't any morning practice, but I'm pretty sure he started something and they just wouldn't let him play. Sucks for him, but that's just too funny," he said, lowering his voice. He slapped my shoulder, smiling.

So that was why he was in the classroom so early. That was calamitous. For Yano.

"So when's he gonna do it?"

"No idea. I mean, it's not like there really is a kaiju."

Didn't seem like I was going to get any more information out of him. It annoyed me a little how flippant he was being, but after thinking about it for a minute, I realized that his attitude was normal. I was the one acting weird.

"You really care that much, Acchi?" Kasai asked. "Don't tell me he's got even you hooked."

"I'm not gonna sneak into the school."

"'Course not, you're too serious."

"That's right, I'm not like you, Kasai."

"Wha?"

His expression suddenly darkened. That happened now and then. It was pretty rare, but occasionally, when I messed with Kasai, he would suddenly make a very unhappy face. Everyone gets pissed off now and then, but seeing that sort of expression on someone as carefree as Kasai made me nervous.

"I mean, uh..."

He laughed then. "Ahaha, seriously man, what is with you, Acchi?"

Kasai smiled wider than before, slapping me again on the shoulder as though he had seen the fear come across on my face and simply found it funny. That calmed me down in a hurry.

It also just so happened that the one person who could always brighten up Kasai's mood was passing by as we left the restroom. It was perfect timing, both for Kasai and for me. It was Midorikawa, who was walking towards the cafeteria. I got the impression that she brought her own lunch every day, but maybe she was on the way to buy some juice or something.

"Yo," Kasai called energetically from behind her. "Midorikawa, you off to the snack counter?"

Despite his enthusiasm, she turned languidly, with no hint of surprise. She nodded with a simple "Mm."

Any normal person, at this point, might have offered up at least a "What about you two?" But if you waited for something like that from Midorikawa, you'd be there until sundown. Perhaps realizing this, or perhaps just wishing to prolong the conversation, Kasai continued to speak, his voice slightly higher than normal.

"By the way, Midorikawa, have you heard? Apparently a kaiju's been showing up around here lately."

Midorikawa tilted her head and said nothing. Her way of saying no. There were times, now and then, when I really wondered whether she could even *say* anything other than "Mm," but she always managed a proper reply when the teachers called on her in class.

"Apparently, there's a kaiju that comes out at night. Honestly, I don't believe it."

"Mm."

"A bunch of people say they've seen it, though. You have any interest in things like that, Midorikawa?"

"Mm."

"Whoa, seriously? I'm surprised, ahaha. Well then, if I hear anything else, I'll let you know."

"Mm."

"Anyway, we're gonna go play soccer. Sorry for interruptin' you."

"Mm," she said, which perhaps meant, "Yes, you did interrupt me." She gave a nod, and, as though she deemed the conversation over, turned her back and left without another word. It seemed awfully rude, but Kasai was grinning and in high spirits, so I guess that was fine.

We finally headed to the entrance, me walking alongside Kasai, whose mood was fully restored. The other guys had already started playing. "C'mon, hurry up!" Kasai demanded, dragging me along. Pretty presumptuous for someone who had caused the delay himself. We arrived quickly at the shoe box designated for our class, finding someone already there.

"Oh hey, Nakagawa. Don't usually see you go outside."

Kasai was already opening the door of his own shoe locker as he spoke to her and perhaps didn't see what Nakagawa was holding in her hands. I did, and realized why she was standing there. Maybe that's why the two of us locked eyes for a moment before I averted my gaze.

"Are you two going to play soccer?" Nakagawa asked, not appearing at all concerned with being caught.

"Yeah. What about you?"

It was then, as Kasai shoved his feet into his athletic shoes and looked up at Nakagawa, that he seemed to finally notice what she was holding in her hands.

"Whoa, what the heck?!"

Nakagawa laughed. It was a pair of shoes, gripped in a cleaning cloth, along with a box cutter.

"I thought it was time for a little payback," she said in a lilting tone, looking from Kasai to me. This time, I averted my gaze in time.

"Ah, those are hers, huh?" I asked.

"That's right!"

Nakagawa seemed overjoyed at my confirmation. It was very much like seeing a princess who had been lauded by her subjects before the eyes of a handsome prince.

I guess she was certain that Yano was the culprit. As I mulled over this conviction, which the rest of the class seemed to agree with, Kasai gave a rather impressed-sounding, "Oh?"

Nakagawa's eyes flicked immediately back to him.

"So, you're sure, then?" he asked.

"Hm?"

"You figured out for sure that she was the one who did that to your shoes?" he asked innocently, putting to words what I could not.

Her lips pursed.

"Well, there's no evidence, but it's obvious, isn't it?"

Evidence, huh? Seemed like a lot of people liked playing detective these days.

It was not at all strange for her to come to this conclusion, given what had happened with Iguchi, I thought, but Kasai did not appear to agree.

"Then it's kinda soon for that, isn't it?"

I don't think that Nakagawa was expecting such a reply. It was surprising even to me. Though he would never do anything to her directly, I assumed that Kasai harbored a deep-seated hatred for Yano. Where he differed from the others in our class was that he didn't hate her out of some herd mentality or a sense of unity or even justice, but because she had hurt someone he cherished, pure and simple. Thus, I figured that he was indifferent to all the things that others did around him.

Doubtless, Nakagawa never thought she would be admonished by a classmate about something regarding Yano—and especially not Kasai. "Y-yes, I guess you're right," she muttered, smiling only with her lips. She dropped Yano's shoes on the spot, passed between us, and left.

Guess she was embarrassed, I thought as I watched her walk away.

"All right, let's get goin'," said Kasai.

"Yeah."

As I followed behind Kasai, I silently thanked him—not for the fact that Yano's shoes had made it out of this unscathed but for chasing Nakagawa away.

To be honest, I had never been very fond of her. Maybe it was because her good looks gave her confidence or something, but she was the kind of person who had no qualms about harming those whom she deemed below her. Even before the class came to hate Yano as a whole, Nakagawa would talk to Yano in that wheedling voice of hers and then make fun of whatever Yano had said with the girls she actually was friends with. Moreover, Yano was not her only target; Iguchi and other weak-willed classmates were all fodder for her ridicule.

All the better that she was hurt by Kasai, I thought, who she thought so highly of. If it hurt her a bit to be admonished, that was for the best, whether she took it as being over her lack of morals or because she'd leapt to conclusions.

When I thought of how Nakagawa's gaze trembled, despite all that bravado of hers, my heart felt just a little bit lighter.

At the same time, I realized how stupid it was for everyone to wish for someone else to get hurt. Instead, I wished for Kasai—who was jovial and emotional but possessed a sharp sense of judgment—to have his prayers finally be heard. In other words, I hoped Midorikawa would have slightly better communication skills from here on out.

The day finished with no other major incident to speak of. The only other things that happened were eraser crumbs being tossed at Yano during class and Takao's missing bike being discovered in the nearby river.

Tuesday NIGHT

As soon as I transformed that night, I rushed to the school. I had no idea when Motoda and his goons planned to show up, which meant that it could happen today. Having a group of boys and one girl all alone in the school at night could become an issue even outside of bullying.

As I arrived at the classroom, thinking how throwing a monster into the mix might only exacerbate things, I found that Yano-san had yet to arrive.

How strange, I thought, since it was already during the time that she referred to as midnight break. Perhaps she was depressed about what had happened during the day and had decided not to come for once. Now that I thought about it, that would be perfectly reasonable. The incident with Iguchi was one thing, but to be pinned as a criminal for a crime that no one could ever prove, to be called out and have accusations tossed at her that no one would even think to take back...

"Wah!"

"Gwahh!!"

As I took my seat in the back of the classroom as always, I was startled by a loud sound from behind and let out a shout. At the same time, the black droplets of my body went flying out as they had once before, knocking over the nearby desks. The violent sound of the chairs striking the floor overlapped with the sound of the cleaning supply cabinet closing.

"Hey."

A few seconds after I called out, the cabinet creaked open. Inside was Yano-san, tittering evilly, her eyes two crescent moons.

I grew immediately annoyed. That was becoming something of a nightly occurrence. And here I had been worrying about her. "Quit it. For all we know those guys might show up today."

"Do you know...when Noto-sensei's birthday...is?"

"Now, look..."

She really needed to be more serious about this, I thought, and then stopped myself. Surely this bad habit of not listening when others spoke had been thoroughly ingrained over the dozen-odd years she had lived up until now. I could see in her eyes that she thought absolutely nothing of my warning.

Still, why on earth was she talking about Noto-sensei's birthday?

"I dunno. How come?"

"It's...next week."

"And how'd you learn when her birthday is?"

"I...asked her. She'll be...thirty-three."

Two things about that surprised me. The first was that Noto-sensei was thirty-three. Kasai had already told me that she was probably around thirty, but I had been thoroughly convinced that she was still in her twenties. And I wasn't the only one—all of the students called her "Non-chan," like it was nothing. The second was that Yano-san was on good enough terms with Noto-sensei to be discussing her birthday with her. Maybe she escaped to the nurse's office to take breaks when she got overwhelmed, like Noto-sensei was always encouraging us to do.

Of course, what one counted as "overwhelmed" was a matter of perspective.

Yano-san clambered out of the supply cabinet and swayed her way over to her seat. Now, we were in our usual positions.

"I was thinking...of giving her...a present."

"Seriously?"

The idea of giving a birthday present to a teacher was shocking, but now that I thought about it, plenty of girls gave chocolates to the young male teachers on Valentine's. It really wasn't all that strange a notion. There was just something very peculiar about the idea of Yano-san being the one to do it.

"Well, I guess that'd be good?"

"Are you...the kind who pushes something you like...on other people...as presents? Or the kind...who gives people things...that *they* like?"

"I'm the type who gives something appropriate that won't cause trouble for them."

"Is appropriate...different from adequate?"

What do you think? I thought, shaking my head side to side. "Appropriate means thinking about how the other person might react and choosing a gift that most people would be a least a little bit happy to receive."

"Hmm... It's hard to...live, when you have to think about so many different...things."

To me, it would be much harder to live without considering all of these things, but that was a topic I was not about to broach.

"I want to try to live...a bit more simply than...that."

"Yano-san...don't you think things would be better if you *did* think about things a little more?"

That much of a warning was appropriate, I felt.

"But then things would...be as hard for me...as they are for you."

"...My life isn't all that hard."

Not like yours, I meant.

"It's fine. Don't worry so...much, Acchi-kun."

No, I had just said that my life wasn't hard. Listen for once. Being needlessly comforted was truly grating.

I tried to make what I thought was a slightly unhappy face, but Yano-san continued.

"Noto-sensei was saying...something."

"What?" I asked.

Still sitting in her chair, facing me, Yano-san patted her chest. Perhaps she was imitating Noto-sensei or something. "Difficult things can be good...for you. Keep on...living. You can live a bit... more freely, once you're an adult."

"..."

"What do...you think? Moving...isn't it?"

Yano-san, reveling in it all, appeared to mistake my silence for deep emotion. It occurred to me that demanding someone be moved was a surefire way to break the mood.

I wasn't silent though. I was dumbfounded that Yano-san had so proudly related those words.

Noto-sensei knew what was going on with Yano-san, and she had given that advice to her. Somehow, she knew all about how Yano-san was treated by the class, what her daily life was like at school.

If she knew, then why hadn't she done anything? Why had she only given her those knowing words, instead of stepping in to save her? She was a teacher, wasn't she? An *adult*.

My whole body shuddered.

"What's...wrong?"

"Nothing," I said.

Honestly, I got it. I understood. If Noto-sensei knew about it, then that probably meant that she *couldn't* interfere. Within the bounds of the classroom, within the bounds of the class, within the bounds of our shared unity, teachers and other adults were outsiders through and through. Those of us on the inside knew that better than anyone else.

Nothing could be done from the outside. If anyone were to meddle, things might just end up much, much worse.

"Are...you hungry?"

"Wait, now that I think about it, doesn't talking about Noto-sensei count as talking about the daytime?"

I offered up her usual retort, forming a grin with my monstrous mouth. Of course, it was not that I actually intended to do her any harm. More than anything, I thought that employing her usual mysterious logic might give me some kind of escape, or maybe she'd pretended not to hear me and I could change the subject or something. Either one would distract her from my silence, so either one was fine.

However...

"It's not a daytime topic, so it's...fine," said Yano-san.

"...What do you mean?"

"C'mon, Acchi-kun, let's fix...the desks. You're the one who knocked them...over, after all. The...poor things."

As usual, she had no interest in actually talking, so I said nothing more, silently fixing up the desks. Yano-san clumsily tried to help, but her hands kept slipping, sending the desks tumbling once again to the ground. Pity the poor furniture that suffered at her hands.

"Be careful. What'll you do if someone hears that noise?"

"Who?"

"The guards, or those other guys, if they came here."

"Isn't it good if the in...vade...ers find us?"

It took me about ten seconds to reconstruct that word in my head into "invaders." Honestly, that seemed like a term better applied to a kaiju.

"You *want* them to find us?"

"If not, then how...will you chase them off, Acchi...kun?"

"Ah, gotcha. If I don't scare them off, they might set up base here."

"Yes...ob...vi...ously."

Seriously?

Unfortunately, she wasn't wrong. I swallowed back the complaint lingering in my throat and pondered the best way to deal with the invaders.

"I'll leave a clone at the front gate, then."

"Your Sha...dow, right? Shadow."

I continued, "When they get here, I'll lure them into the building and then come after them."

"Sounds...good."

I quickly prepared a clone and sent it to the gate. This one couldn't change its size or breathe fire. Furthermore, if I sent him outside of the gates, he would vanish—perhaps because I had only envisioned him as being useful within the school, the first time.

"Come to...think of it, who was that, yester...day?" Yano-san asked.

The question came so abruptly that it took me a moment to process what she was talking about.

"Oh yeah, the one who set off the alarm in the courtyard?"

"May...be some idiot from our...class."

As I wondered why Yano-san would assume that, I recalled something—though I didn't do it of my own volition.

"Nakagawa-san was saying that someone threw her shoes out into the yard. Maybe whoever was here yesterday dropped them."

"That's day...time...talk."

"But them dropping them might've happened at night," I pointed out.

Yano-san fell silent despite her initial protest, as though having accepted this explanation. I ignored her immediate, childish reply of, "Can you...prove it?"

"If it is someone from our class, I wonder who."

"Someone who hates Yuri...ko-chan."

By Yuriko-chan she meant Nakagawa. When I thought about the people who hated her, a single human immediately came to mind. Not a monster, a *human*.

"What's your de...duction, De...tective Acchi-kun?"

Though I couldn't make anything approaching a "deduction," I at least knew that the culprit wasn't me, so I had to start with considering the retreating form I had seen the night before. The person was short, though not as short as Yano-san, with hair that did not extend past their shoulders.

"A boy, like Kasai..." I said.

"Could've been a...girl."

"There are no girls in our class that height with hair that short."

"Maybe they...cut it. Well then, Acchi-kun, your conclu...sion is that it's Kasai...kun?"

"Mm, I mean, I don't think he'd have done it."

"Why...not?"

"He's not that kind of person."

Yano-san didn't know much about Kasai. I tried to explain to her that he didn't have a wicked bone in his body. Naturally, I omitted the parts about what Nakagawa-san had been trying to do, and Kasai's feelings for Midorikawa. Yano-san at least knew that Kasai never participated in harming her, so my image of him seemed to jive with her impressions.

As I continued giving my one-sided exposition, Yano-san sighed. "Hm...hmm. He really is...smooth," she said.

I wasn't sure what she meant by "smooth."

"And he's...smart, too."

"Actually, his grades suck. He doesn't like thinking too hard about things."

"That's about what I...imagined," she continued. She sounded dissatisfied, despite not being much of a decent judge of anything. Despite knowing nothing about Kasai. She added, "He seems... like the kind of person who could never...ever fall for...anyone."

See? She knew nothing at all.

"Not like you, Acchi...kun," she said.

"...I really have no idea what you're talking about."

"I'm talking...about Igu...chan. The one you...like."

Uninterested in all this mushy talk, I quickly reached for a change of subject. "Why don't we go see what the library's like at night?" Even if those guys showed up, there were plenty of places where we could hide there, and it wouldn't take us much time to get there from here.

I'd only proposed it as a way to kill time, but Yano-san's response was, "Sounds...hella lame."

"I don't want to hear that from you," I spat, to which Yano-san replied, "That was a com...pliment."

And just what about it was complimentary, exactly?

Despite the disagreement, eventually the two of us decided to head to the library. We followed the same procedure as always upon exiting the room—me unlocking and then relocking the door.

"I was thinking that it might be...Kudou...chan." We walked down the hallway, her voice as thoughtlessly loud as always.

"She's not that sort of person, either."

"Hm...hmm. Like I said, Acchi...kun. Hella...lame."

Finally, it occurred to me that she was baiting me, and when I realized that I was falling for it, I managed to calm down. Getting riled up was exactly what Yano-san wanted out of me.

As we approached the library, Yano-san went galloping in. I followed behind at a measured pace, impeded by my own sense of decorum. Like the nurse's office, the library—which I hadn't visited in a while—had a scent all of its own, different from the rest of the school. This unique atmosphere, the smell and the silence of the night, it all gave my spirits a gentle lift.

Whenever I happened to come here, I couldn't help but think of a particular classmate of ours, but I did not broach the subject. It was a daytime topic, after all, best left alone.

"Oh, there's Harry...Potter."

I looked to where she indicated and saw the series on prominent display. There it was, proof positive that reading Harry Potter wasn't weird—I found myself relieved.

Yano-san began to wander all about the library. After a few minutes, I realized how much of a chore it was to follow her and decided to wait by the entrance instead. If anyone showed up, I'd be in the perfect position to scare them off and settle the matter.

So far, I hadn't seen any disturbance through the eyes of my clone waiting at the gate. It seemed that this was to be a quiet night after all. Everyone loves a little peace and quiet after dark.

Gazing into the darkened library, I suddenly got the feeling that it had reached a certain point in the night. Sure enough, I soon heard the alarm from Yano-san's phone jingling from a corner of the library. I saw Yano-san herself poke her head out through a gap in the shelves before she came trotting back over.

"Didn't see...anything I wanted to read," she said.

"Didn't you say you don't read books, anyway?"

"Yeah, but you said there were some in...teresting ones out there...too."

Though I didn't show it on my face, I was surprised. I couldn't recall saying such a thing, nor could I believe that she would actually accept it.

"But the books...that are just all full of words...don't seem very in...teresting."

"You can't judge books at a single glance like that."

"I *like* things that you can judge...at just a glance."

Tell that to the ones making the books, I thought, standing, ushering her to the exit ahead of me. I locked the door in the usual fashion.

"Hm?"

"What's...up?"

"When we came in, you went in before me."

"Yeah?"

"Was it locked?"

"Nope."

Maybe someone forgot to lock it. The guards would probably be back to lock it later. I recalled my clone from the gates and proceeded down to the entrance with my usual firm caution. Along the way, Yano-san hummed to herself, truly devoid of any sense of self-preservation. When I warned her about this, she replied in a singsong voice. "Igu-chan's gonna hate you...if you're always so fussy." This earned her a second warning, that the next day I would be bringing a towel or something so I could shut her up by force without directly touching her if I needed to.

Yes, I would be seeing her again, same time tomorrow.

"See you tomorrow," I said, moving through the gate.

"Okay," she replied, nodding with a weirdly serious look upon her face.

I secretly followed her as she tottered home on her bike, worried about what might happen if she encountered those boys en route. For the first time, I realized just how close her house was to mine. It was an average, garden-variety house.

Not that I ever had any intention of going there.

Wednesday
DAY

TODAY, AS ALWAYS, Yano-san's "Good...morning" went ignored. Some of our classmates had begun to believe that she was responsible not only for Nakagawa's missing shoes, but also for stealing Takao's bike, and everyone sneered to see her digging through the garbage in the morning. Seeing Nakagawa hurt had only strengthened the sense of unity between the girls of our class. However, there was at least one blessing from Yano's rapidly deteriorating circumstance.

The necessary conditions had finally been fulfilled.

"Tonight?" I said. "That's pretty sudden."

Though I was thankful to Kasai for providing this intel, I was racked with nerves and let my true thoughts slip.

"Yeah. I'll be busy playing games, so I told him not to bother calling me."

Right. As far as Kasai was concerned, that time of night was always booked solid for gaming. Yano and Motoda weren't the only ones in our class who could be seen nodding off in the middle of the day.

"You find out what's up for me, Acchi," he said.

"I'll be asleep."

"Guess so. You've always been a real early-bird type, huh?"

He heaved a sigh and then smiled warmly at me, resigned. I couldn't tell if it was because he had accepted this as a quirk of mine or if this was a smile of pure exasperation, but either way it seemed that he had forgiven me. I felt relieved.

"Anyway, I guess either the kaiju won't show, and then they just go home, or else they'll catch it, which is a whole new can of worms. It'd be a lot cooler if they caught it though, ahaha."

I laughed along with Kasai, who was probably imagining what it would look like if Motoda and the others caught me. I continued to laugh along, even as he said, laughing, "Apparently he hurt that first-year pretty bad, and now he's on suspension."

This was not the time for me to be worrying about the injuries of people I didn't know. The final battle was tonight.

As I watched Iguchi walking a firm distance away from Yano after cooking class, unlike last week, my resolve grew firm.

Wednesday NIGHT

*I*T FEELS LIKE there have been countless times in my life where I've been at the mercy of Murphy's law—though perhaps it's only that I'm more inclined to remember the times when things go wrong, while the good times slip my mind.

Tonight was just one of those nights.

Tonight, on the night when Motoda and company were supposed to be sneaking into the school, already twenty minutes into Yano-san's midnight break, I was still at home—in my house, in my room, and still in human form, pacing a hole into the floor.

"C'mon, c'mon, *c'mon*," I chanted quietly to myself, but the black drops were not forthcoming—on this night of *all* nights!

This was bad. According to Kasai, they would be showing up around the same time that Motoda had spotted the monster before, which meant that it wouldn't be surprising if they were already inside of the school.

Maybe I ought to have already started making my way to school while still in human form. Then again, it would be much worse for someone to see me transforming along the way.

Thinking maybe there might be some problem with my stance or something, I tried lying down, then squatting, then sitting, but there was no transformation in sight. The worst-case scenario, which had never occurred to me before, floated through my mind.

What if I had already used up all of my transformations?

Though that seemed impossible, if it were the case, I would have no choice but to accept it. Given that I had no idea why I was even transforming into a monster in the first place, it wouldn't be all that strange for the transformations to just as suddenly stop.

Wondrous things are only wondrous when you still wonder about them. Mysteries should remain mysteries.

Monsters were born shrouded in mystery, and they would vanish just the same.

Which would be great—any *other* day than today!

I tried to remember the first night that I had turned into a monster. What had I done to bring on the transformation then? Black droplets had suddenly started falling from my mouth. I was startled at first, frightened, with no idea what was happening to me. I thought it was a dream.

However much it had felt like a dream, it was not one.

It was only because of that serious streak I possessed, the one Kasai-san had so helpfully pointed out, that I accepted it so readily. What did I lose, if I became a monster after dark? There wasn't anything there for me in the night, nothing I needed to protect.

Things were different for Yano-san. The night was her refuge. And the night could be lost.

I was sure she was there, waiting for me.

Was it okay to leave this a mystery? Not to know?

That couldn't...

"*Ah*... There it is."

Quite suddenly, the transformation began. This time, the black droplets spread from my fingertips, across my whole body, as though I was being eaten alive by ants.

I opened up the window and flew out before my transformation was even finished. I had faith in my monstrous self. The droplets shifted around my body almost frantically, and the next moment, I was soaring in streamlined form.

I rushed to the school. It felt like my speed was rising higher and higher, but perhaps it was just my imagination.

Even on this harrowing night, the night wind felt good brushing past each of the black droplets.

Far faster than normal—now that I think about it, perhaps it was only a few seconds—I arrived at the school. I quickly formed a clone and sent it to the building where the guard room was located, and I headed for the block where my own classroom was.

The door of the entryway had been left open slightly.

Was it by Yano-san? Or by the others?

Putting that question aside, I steeled myself for battle, and flung myself into the darkened school building.

It'll be fine, I assured myself, it'll be fine. Anyone would run if they saw a monster.

So it would be fine.

I stayed in my larger form, in case I bumped into anyone unexpectedly. I wanted to be ready at a moment's notice.

I began quietly creeping along. My clone hadn't spotted anything as of yet.

First, I would head for the classroom. If those guys did run into Yano-san, if they had found her... Well, I honestly hadn't considered what they might do after that, but it definitely wouldn't be pretty.

I climbed to the third floor, doing my best kaiju impression as I proceeded down the hall. I squared my shoulders and held my tail higher than usual—though I have no idea if it was as frightening as I imagined. Step by step, I approached the classroom, glancing inside just before entering, but I saw no one within. I typically snuck in through the back, but wanting to see if Yano-san had arrived, this time I tried the front door.

The door opened with a shrill squeal. Yano-san was here. I always wondered how it was that she managed the lock, but now was not the time to bring that up. I timidly stepped inside and knocked my tail twice on one of the nearby desks.

"Come...in."

I was immediately relieved to hear that insipid reply, but just as quickly felt the urge to make my displeasure known. "Idiot," I muttered, approaching the cleaning supply cabinet.

"What would you have done if that wasn't me?"

She replied with two knocks of her own, rather than speaking. Just what was the point of doing so now?

"Apparently, they're coming tonight," I said. "You should hide yourself."

Hearing one more knock, I locked the front door, and slipped out into the hallway. Were they not here yet? My clone still hadn't spotted anything. It would be best if I could face them down at the gates.

I might as well try looking upstairs, I thought, moving to the stairwell, slowly and quietly.

Now that I thought about it, Motoda had been going on about catching a kaiju, but that was surely just a bit of pretext. Surely those guys had a healthy skepticism about there being a monster. Maybe they didn't believe it at all and were just sneaking into the school for the fun of it. Actually finding a kaiju would be nothing more than an added bonus. All in all, it couldn't be that difficult to scare them off.

Honestly, if they did catch a kaiju, what did they intend to do with it? Keep it as a pet? Kill it? Sell it?

This was a kaiju we're talking about, right? A friggin' *monster*. Just what could a bunch of kids do to me? There was no way I could lose to them. No way that I, at night, in my element, could ever lose to a bunch of guys who had nothing but their measly arm strength to boast of.

"Huh?"

It was on the fifth floor that I came face-to-face with a boy, exiting the bathroom by the stairs.

I held back the cry I was about to let out. I hadn't paid any attention to the sound of water from the bathroom at all, assuming it was just some automatic cleaning system.

"Bwuh?! *Aaaaaaaaaaaah!!!*"

The boy proved slightly less talented at holding back his scream. As I recalled, he was one of Kasai's friends from the baseball team. I summoned up all my strength, body and mind. I shook my form and opened my mouth, evoking the night that I had scared off that stray dog—and roared.

Even to me, my voice sounded sharp, unnatural, more like the sound of aluminum foil being crushed than any sound made by a living being, and the boy was knocked onto his rear end.

Good. He was frightened.

I glared at the boy, still scrambling backwards on his backside, speechless. Then I heard a sound from behind me. As I turned to look, the door of the music room opened, revealing two people staring at me, dumbfounded. It was Motoda and a guy from the next class over. I decided to disregard for now the fact that the music room had been unlocked.

So, there were three of them?

I just had to frighten this trio, so that they would never come near this place again. That was my mission. I silently burned it into my mind. Without hesitation, I leapt over the boy who'd fallen, getting all three of them into my field of vision. The one on the ground let out another shriek, rolling.

As I let out a low growl, the fallen one managed to get to his feet, tripped over himself, and fled toward the stairs that I had just come up. Scaring him off was just what I wanted, but it seemed like it would be more fun to dispatch all three of them at once.

"Eek!"

Just then, my clone arrived from below. As the clone approached the scrambling one from the stairs, I advanced from behind him, trapping the three boys between us. Having them shut themselves up in the music room would be a bother.

Leaving my clone to keep an eye on them, I leapt out the window, slipped around into the music room, and locked the door. Hearing a miserable, almost girlish voice stammering behind me, I leapt back outside.

Going straight back out into the hallway from here would hardly be exciting.

I was sure that the guards would merely think that this was all a dream. Out in the courtyard, I enlarged myself to a size that would truly be worthy of a "kaiju," glaring in at the boys through a window with my elevated gaze.

For a moment, it was so quiet that time seemed to stop. Then, from within, there was a scream. I watched and laughed as the three boys tried to run, terror on their faces, looking like they might crumble at any moment. Naturally, I did so in a monstrous cry, careful not to let out any hint of my human voice.

In order to guide them to the stairs, I left the clone where he was and slipped back into the building myself. They'd go exactly where I wanted, whether they wanted to or not. Partway down, Mr. Backside tripped and tumbled on the landing. I menaced them from the floor above, skulking like a beast stalking prey. Meanwhile, I sent my clone running to the floor below, halting Motoda and the other on the fourth floor.

"Stay back!"

Mr. Backside scrambled again to his feet and rushed to the fourth floor, joining back up with the rest of his party. My clone glared at them from the hallway while I glared at them from the stairs, leaving them a clear path to the third floor and making it obvious to the intruders where they could run.

Was there no special technique I could think of here to threaten them? I growled again, pondering, when there came the harsh sound of Motoda clicking his tongue.

"There's *two* of them?" I thought I heard him mutter, when suddenly he did something unbelievable.

He took the bat that he had been gripping with his left hand the whole time into his right and went swinging at the clone.

"Take that!"

Not knowing what might happen if the clone were to take a hit, I had it back up while I shook my body intimidatingly at him. Seeing this full display of anger, Motoda took a step back. As he did so, both I and the clone each advanced in turn, closing in around him.

What was with this guy? Though I would never show it, the heart I wasn't quite sure I had felt like it was thundering in my chest.

Seriously, to just go swinging at a monster when you didn't even know the extent of its power? Motoda returned to his two companions and readied his bat again. He seemed to come to a conclusion based on the fact that the clone had avoided his swing, not attacked in return, and conversely how the attack appeared to anger me. He smiled his usual unpleasant grin, looked towards the clone, and muttered, "That one must be its kid."

Though his declaration was both incorrect and absurd, for my purposes it was perhaps rather useful. I knew exactly what it was he intended to do next.

"Take that!"

Once again, Motoda swung the bat towards the clone, and when the clone dodged, he swung again, just as I suspected he might. He was exactly the sort of person who would happily attack what he identified as the weakest enemy. He stared at the clone, who he had determined to be a child, with the exact same expression as when he looked at Yano-san during the day.

Avoiding his attacks was no problem. If I needed to, I could run away too fast for them to ever catch me. The other two behind Motoda were frozen in place. Thus, there were only two real problems here.

First off, Motoda had realized that the clone was not going to return his attacks. Truth be told, I had been commanding the clone to smack his bat away, but the clone had not budged. Perhaps it was because I hadn't imbued it with the image of attacking the first time that I summoned it.

Second, I couldn't allow them to touch my main form. I still had no idea what would happen if they did. The tables would be turned on me if the black drops were to turn Motoda into a monster as well.

What was with this guy?! I'd never imagined Motoda would be so reckless! As the clone retreated farther and farther back,

I had no choice but to show them that I had full intention to strike.

Recalling that night on the roof, I ignited the black droplets within me, with a far more restrained image than before, opened my mouth, and let out a small flame. Carefully, *carefully*, so as not to burn them.

"Wah!"

The other two boys had been watching Motoda fight the clone. Feeling the heat from the flame, they jumped back from me. It was apparently effective, as they went running over to Motoda.

"It can breathe fire!"

"Dude, this is bad!"

"We gotta get outta here!"

I continued to close the gap, inch by inch, as they shouted, forming a pincer of sorts with my clone. Of course, the clone was still capable only of defense, so it wasn't as if I could keep this up forever. I needed them to scamper off home.

I maybe got a bit careless from there, frantic in my execution.

I should have had my clone pop outside, and come back over to me, but I underestimated my enemy. Just as Motoda's attack stance seemed to slacken, I instead made the clone leap towards me, up over the three boys' heads.

I really hadn't expected Motoda to be so thoughtless.

I don't know if he knew what the clone was going to do, but he almost reflexively tossed the bat in my direction. The bat arced towards me, so close that it nearly struck the other two boys, and to my dismay, grazed the tail of my clone.

The clone vanished instantaneously, like smoke. Then, one of the fluorescent lamps in the hallway shattered, making an impressive sound. For a moment, it felt as though time stopped.

"...Crapcrapcrapcrapcrap!" Mr. Backside babbled, dashing in the opposite direction from me.

I felt exactly the same way. *Oh crap.*

Besides me, he seemed to be the only one here with a honed sense of danger. As I faced down the other two, something cold, like sweat, dripped down my skin. It was bad that the lamp had shattered. However, I was far more concerned that they had seen that my clone could be defeated with a weapon. I couldn't assume that such an attack wouldn't also work on me. In fact, it was possible that *anything* that struck me with ill intent could have an effect.

In other words, even if I sent them packing tonight, there was a chance that they might come back to the school some other night to hunt me again.

Perhaps I could strike them over the head with something and knock them unconscious? No, I had never directly attacked anything with this body and had no idea how to regulate my strength. I had no idea what I'd do if I accidentally killed them.

As this debate ran through my head, I decided to summon up another clone in the meantime. And yet, it would not come. Was there some sort of restriction to the ability?

I couldn't let them underestimate me. I was a monster. I should be feared.

I roared louder than before, letting a font of flame pour from my mouth, putting on a show of anger that my companion had been dispatched.

"Yo, we need to get out of here!" said the boy from the neighboring class to Motoda, taking a step back. Motoda took a step back as well but persisted in glaring at me.

"Betcha we can get rid of that one too, can't we?"

"Wh-what the hell're you saying?! If we don't get outta here, the guards're gonna show!"

I couldn't let myself fall a step behind them. So, before they could run, I took a step forward and let out an earsplitting battle roar. A noise *that* loud was sure to bring the guards rushing in, and if they dealt with the intruders, then that was good enough for me.

Apparently I'd made the right move. Perhaps assuming that the monster before them was truly enraged, the boys began to run away from me.

I expanded my body to fit just within the width of the hallway and gave chase. I was careful to regulate my pace, just quick enough that they couldn't escape me but just slow enough that I would never catch up. I opened my mouth as I crept behind them on my six feet, driving them down.

Still in good form, they began to run faster. In a sharp showing of split-second decision-making, when they reached the end of the building, they swiftly changed course, heading for the stairs. I leaned my body into the turn and followed suit.

My tail swayed back and forth, smacking against the walls.

The repeated sound of it caused one of them, the boy from the neighboring class, to thoughtlessly turn halfway around to look. He was between the fourth and third floors when his foot missed the last step just before the landing and he stumbled. I leapt to avoid him in the nick of time, clinging to the window that was pouring moonlight down into the stairwell. Only the emergency light now remained to shine its eerie green light.

"Hey—wait a—!!"

Before I bothered determining whether his words were addressed at Motoda or at me, I crawled along the ceiling, and turned about to glare at him. Seeing a monster defy gravity was sure to be unsettling.

It would have been splendid if this was enough to frighten them, but this was not the case. Motoda stared at me, half-turned, making no moves to run.

Just then, my vision was assailed by a bright light.

"Oi! Run!"

The voice was coming from the boy from the next class over. When I looked in the direction of the sound, spots dancing before my eyes, I saw a phone in his hand. The light must have come from that. Seriously, dude? This wasn't an anime or a game—you couldn't just assume that bright light would pierce through a shadowy monster. That said, it was still effective against *me*—the human somewhere inside.

I had to scare them once more before I could let them run, I thought. I dropped to the floor to chase them down into the hallway, my eyes still stinging. I would keep chasing them down to the first floor, then let a big fireball out on the grounds, and that ought to finally be enough.

Or so I thought, but the pair were not so kind as to abide by my assumptions.

"C'mon," said Motoda, running not towards the stairs but towards the hallway. Realizing that the command was directed towards him, the other boy scampered after him, a few beats behind. I followed.

Just what was his game? What in the world did he intend to do?

As I followed them, roaring, Motoda passed by one empty classroom, then another, finally putting his hand on the front door of the room occupied by our class.

A momentary tremor ran through me, but it was fine, I had remembered to lock the door that Yano-san had unlocked somehow. *Ka-chak*, it went—the sound of the lock properly doing its job.

"Damn it, what the *hell?!*"

I wasn't quite sure what Motoda had been expecting. He cussed at the door and took off running again. I chased behind until I had very nearly caught him, opening my mouth as though to swallow him whole.

There was nothing to obstruct my open mouth.

Undaunted by his failure, Motoda ran and laid a hand on the back door. *Doing the same thing over and over and expecting a different result is a mark of insanity,* I thought to myself, and was instantly betrayed when the door opened.

The two slipped inside the classroom as I, still running, passed them by.

How? Just as the question crossed my mind, I heard the sound of the lock clicking shut.

It hadn't even occurred to me, because we always went through the front door. Had Yano-san unlocked the back door, too? Why? And why had Motoda run straight to the classroom as though he knew?

Panicking, I turned around and stared into the classroom through the window. The two of them stared back at me, sweat dripping down their faces.

Meanwhile, my body rippled with nerves. Yano-san was hiding in the supply cabinet just behind them. If they found her, it was all over.

It was just as I finished the thought that it happened. Almost immediately, I saw the door of the supply cabinet open, and Yano-san peeked out, grinning smugly, perhaps to ascertain what was going on.

Are you stupid?! I wanted to curse but held back. I needed to keep their attention on me.

As always, I put a certain image in my mind. Unlike always, however, I did so slowly, carefully, so as to draw out my enemies' fears.

I scattered myself like liquid and poured into the classroom through a crack in the doorway. Bit by tiny bit, the black droplets seeped into the classroom, like a cauldron bubbling over, like a poison gas spreading.

The pair were frozen still. No doubt they'd never imagined that I might make my way into the room like this. As I reformed my body into a smaller thing than it had been out in the hall, I heard a scream.

What do you think, boys? Didn't think I could do that, did ya? I thought cruelly, laughing through my monstrous mouth.

"What is *with* this thing?!" shouted Motoda, seizing the chair closest to him and chucking it my way. I grabbed it up with my tail and tossed it gently right back, as gently as when I had handed Yano-san the umbrella. This was merely to show them that I was capable of touching objects directly.

Somehow, though stunned, Motoda caught the chair, looking hatefully towards me.

"You messin' with me?"

He must have assumed I was toying with my prey, though in reality, I didn't have that sort of luxury anymore. Frightening them off for good without being able to actually *touch* them had turned out more challenging than I expected. But if Motoda thought the predator had made him into a plaything? That suited my purposes just fine.

After all, that was what he always did to others.

My body was roiling now with something other than nerves. I couldn't take my time here. I needed them to leave the classroom before they could discover Yano-san. I couldn't just scare them out onto the balcony and have them jump. This was the third floor, after all.

As I considered how I could scare them away, my opponent made his move. Motoda grabbed Kudou's bamboo sword from kendo club, which lay above the lockers we all used, turned toward me, and readied himself.

Crap, I thought staring down the wooden blade. But it wasn't Motoda's battle stance that unnerved me—it was the fact that I saw his companion behind him, looking for a weapon so he could take up arms against me alongside Motoda. Never once taking his eyes off me, he reached slowly in the direction of the cleaning supply cabinet. Perhaps he thought that I wouldn't notice.

What could I do? My heart and my brain were on fire. I needed to act, and yet I stood there, overthinking what my next move should be, and so I acted too late.

His hand reached the handle of the cabinet. Twice his fingers swept past it, but the third time he took hold and gently tried to open it.

However, the cabinet didn't open. Yano-san was probably barring it from within. Just when I thought I could finally be at ease, however...

"Some...one's...in here!"

Before I could shout, *How stupid can you be?!* the two boys jumped, trying to distance themselves from the cabinet from which they had suddenly heard a high-pitched voice. This was a boon to me. I swallowed back my scream and leapt over to the cabinet. This was it.

It all happened in the blink of an eye, so I couldn't say that I had recalled Yano-san's words or anything like that.

I opened my mouth up wide and chomped down with all my might onto the supply cabinet.

And then, I imagined.

Inside my body was a universe. A vast space was unfurling inside of me, greater than could be seen from outside. My mouth was the entrance to this space from which I could swallow up anything I chose. Those things would lie within me, and I could spit them back out whenever I wanted.

In a matter of seconds, I swallowed the supply cabinet up whole, like a bird swallowing a fish. I completed this task without even having the freedom to doubt whether I actually could, looking the two flabbergasted boys in the eye.

Once again, it felt as though time stopped.

"*Waaaaaaaaaaaaah!!!*"

Apparently, seeing a monster swallow up something larger than them had given them quite the shock. The pair screamed and then rushed from the classroom, tripping over themselves.

With the power of imagination, anything is possible.

Of course, I had no reason to believe such a thing, but the question was always in the back of my mind: *But what if I could?* What if I could sprout wings and fly? What if I could sink into the ground? What if I could teleport? And from out of those flights of fancy came a pocket dimension. Though of course, I was a monster. Swallowing things up was just what we did.

And yet, I had never truly tested my power, still afraid of hearing those words.

If you can do anything, then rescue me.

No matter what power I had, that was not something I could do.

That said, at least during the nighttime, I would do all that I could. If I didn't, that idiot would wind up revealing herself. That was exactly how hopeless she was.

At the very least, tonight, this monster could rescue her.

After standing the bamboo sword that Motoda had so violently tossed up against the shelf, I decided to give chase. I needed to at least force them off of the school grounds.

It was easy enough to pursue them as they tripped down the stairs. As I gave a roar from behind to let them know of my presence, the pair glanced back, let out a scream, and then ran with all they had.

I looked at Motoda, who cried pitifully, "Stay back!"

This was starting to get fun.

When they reached the first floor, the pair sensibly ran straight for the entrance and then directly outside. It was here that I realized that, unlike Yano-san, they had not bothered to change into their indoor shoes when sneaking in.

Now that we were outdoors, I could finally change myself to a size of my liking.

I found them running for the gate. As if he had been kindly awaiting the other two, Mr. Backside was there as well.

I vibrated my body up to a properly kaiju-like size and placed my first step down just where the trio were about to tread. With the writhing black drops as a cushion, the motion made no sound but still kicked up dust off of the ground.

They continued to the gates, falling over themselves at least twice. Now, for my insurance policy. Very carefully, making sure that no one was around, I breathed flames in the direction they were running. Just as I pictured it, a path of fire stretched until just beyond the gate, leaving them no route but the one by which they might escape. They rolled on the ground and looked up at me, eventually growing motionless. Was it simply too hot for them? They couldn't even stand, it seemed.

As I stood there, puzzled by their sudden cowardice, Motoda screamed something.

I strained my ears to listen. It sounded like a curse. He was peering at me, wide-eyed. "Damn it! Just what the hell are you?!"

Your classmate, I obviously could not reply.

"We weren't even doing anything!"

Sure, they hadn't done anything...yet. But once again, I could not reply. Instead, I stamped my foot once, a warning that I could crush them at any moment.

Though I had countless times now shown them just what my shifting forms could do, Motoda persisted in his bluff, glaring daggers up at me despite the fear plain on his face.

Just then, as I felt my irritation rising, he said something he should not have.

"What d'you want with my school?!"

Suddenly, the brain that I was not certain was inside of me reached its boiling point.

"...It isn't yours."

There was no way to label the words but a mistake. I have no excuse. They just slipped out of me. By the time I cursed myself for it, it was already too late. Motoda appeared to have heard me loud and clear. He was frozen, his eyes open wide.

It's all over, I thought. He heard my voice. They knew that I was a monster now.

However, the reason that I thought this was because I was inadvertently using Yano-san as the standard by which to judge our other classmates.

"You can talk…?" I was relieved to hear him squeak out those words. Of course. Of *course* that was the part he'd focus on. Who wouldn't be surprised to learn that a monster who looked like me possessed the intelligence to use words? Or that they could *understand* those words? No one would be stupid enough to focus on figuring out just whose voice it was, especially not the first time they heard it.

"O-okay, I get it!" he shouted.

He got what?

"I won't come back! I won't come back again!"

Though he spoke as though prostrating himself before me, Motoda managed to clamber to his feet and began to run, leaving his companions behind. Somehow or other the boy from the next class made it to his feet as well. He ran behind, shouting, "Wait!"

It seemed that they hadn't interpreted my words the way I meant them. To them, it probably appeared that I was the master of this school or something. Well, if so, that was good enough for my purposes. That meant that they would never return here at night.

With the speed that only a group of athletes could possess, the intruders were gone in the blink of an eye. I drew in as much air as I could into the lungs that I wasn't certain I possessed and let out a sigh.

Apparently, it was all over.

Still a seeming kaiju, I looked up to the heavens. All the tension that had seized my body melted away.

Thank goodness. I had won. I'd chased them away. Motoda and the rest.

Suddenly, my whole body seized with a particular emotion, and once more I thought something that showed that very childishness Iguchi had accused me of.

I really was invincible at night.

With the power of imagination, I could even create a whole universe, I began to think, when I suddenly remembered the one who was still inside of me. Goodness, she could be drowning in there.

I had no clue what would happen to things within my body once I swallowed them. If it was as I imagined it, it would be like wandering around in space. At first, I thought I might head for the classroom, but after reconsidering, I decided to head up to the roof. The force exerted in spitting her back up might break a window or something, which would be bad news. I had already broken that one fluorescent light as it was.

I leapt up high, changed myself into a comfortable sitting size while still midair, and landed upon the rooftop. As I tried to cough the supply cabinet up as quickly as possible, I suddenly grew uneasy.

What if, because I had imagined the interior of my body to be like outer space, she had asphyxiated and died from the lack of oxygen? What if there was a black hole somewhere inside of me, and the whole cabinet had been crushed up to pieces?

There was no point in sitting here getting frightened. I was going to have to bring it back up sometime. I summoned up my courage, along with the image of carefully spitting the cabinet out from my mouth. At last, from the depths of my mouth, the rectangular box emerged, parting the black droplets as it came. I was immediately relieved to see that it at least had not been crushed.

Before I spat the whole thing out, I supported it with my tail, standing it upright on the roof so that it wouldn't fall over. I doubt the supply cabinet had any plans of coming up here to the roof, either.

Now came the worry of whether or not Yano-san was breathing.

I stood before the supply cabinet, which looked eerie in the moonlight. After several seconds of waiting, with no apparent activity from inside the cabinet, I gripped the handle with my tail and tentatively opened the door. Inside was Yano-san, standing straight up, frozen, her eyes closed.

Was she...actually dead?

As I looked upon her, growing increasingly worried, her eyes suddenly popped open. They opened with such force that you could practically hear the sound effect. I jumped in shock. After blinking numerous times, she took a step out, and her lips pursed.

"Oo," she said.

"...Oo?" I repeated.

"Ooo."

"..."

What was she trying to say? I took a step forward, straining my ears.

"Ooo...oooo...ooooo...oooooo*waaaaahhh!!!*"

Out of nowhere, she raised a battle cry.

Not at all prepared for such a loud sound, my body swelled in proportion with the distress inside my heart.

Utterly unconcerned for me, once she had expended all the air in her little body, Yano-san took another deep breath and once more opened her mouth in a "Wah" shape.

"*Waaaaaaaaaaaaaaahhh!!!*"

This time she started hopping around the rooftop, still spewing out a scream that sounded like a broken toy. She wore her usual self-satisfied grin, and I worried that she had finally gone mad from being swallowed up by a monster. However, I somehow realized that was not the case.

"That was...crazy! So...effin'...crazy!"

She took off suddenly, running around in circles.

"I thought...they'd found me!" she burbled, still grinning as she run up to me, both hands outstretched. "You ate me all up!"

"Quiet! Keep it down!"

My voice was probably plenty loud too as I scolded her, but Yano-san kept on raising her voice, as if drawing a circle with it.

"That was soooo scary!"

I twitched. She hadn't heard me at all.

"*Yano-san.*"

"What?! What?!"

"I was the one who was scared! Why would you show your face?! Why would you talk?!"

"Yeah...seriously!"

"Don't just *agree* with me!"

Perhaps reading the exasperation on my face, she began to sway restlessly, an even more amused smile on her face. Back and forth, back and forth.

Suddenly, something within me burst. I don't know why— surely I was utterly dumbfounded by her behavior, on top of my existing agitation.

"Seriously, what is *with* you?"

Even I realized that there was not a hint of actual malice behind my words. I think I had genuinely begun to take some sort of strange interest in this even stranger classmate of mine.

The fact that we had made it out of this safely only meant that we would have to be even more resolute, more cautious, if there was to be a next time. But there was no need for such things at the moment. So, it was fine to bask in our victory for now. I could understand why Yano-san might be in the mood to revel.

I watched silently as Yano-san leapt and bounded and danced a strange step like a hyperactive child. Finally, she stopped in place, as though having expended all the excess energy in her body, her shoulders heaving with breath as she stared at her hands for some reason.

"That was...so...exciting."

"So I figured."

"I was really...scared."

"...You're weird, you know that, Yano-san?"

Yano-san tilted her head at my friendly ribbing, her shoulders shaking with ragged breath.

"What's...weird?"

I pointed at her with my tail. "What do you mean, 'what?' It's you. *You're* weird."

"No, I'm...not."

No matter how you looked at it, the outrageous way she shook her head back and forth was incredibly odd. I laughed again. "I mean like, back in the classroom, and now."

"Hm...hmm?"

"That face of yours."

Caught up in the mood, I let one of my most persistent thoughts slip.

"My face?"

"Even when you're talking about how scared you were, you've still got that big smile on your face. It's super weird!" I said, teasing, only a little malice behind it. She should be able to accept at least this much of a jab as payback for making me worry so much, I figured. It was the sort of thing you would say to a friend, not taking into account things like whether or not it would hurt them.

For a moment, she was stunned. She put her hands to her face and muttered, "Aa...aa...ahhh." Then she explained, as though there was something she had forgotten to mention this whole time. "So...I..."

She moved the hands that had been pressed to her cheeks towards her mouth.

"I can't help...it, but when I...get scared, I al...ways...smile."

Then, she pushed up both corners of her mouth.

"Sort of...like this, all...sm...ug...ly."

Ugly?

"...Huh?" I said.

Oh. Satisfied. *Smugly.*

She pushed the edges of her mouth all the way to their limits.

There it was. Her usual smile. That strange smile that I saw every single day.

"I guess it's a ha...bit. I'm...always doing that...huh?" she said, squishing her own cheeks.

Always.

At any given time?

I thought over what she was saying, my brain on fire. It felt as though the night wind had suddenly blown away all the sense of triumph within me.

"What?" I asked.

She was grinning smugly, here, right before my eyes.

She grinned when Motoda struck her with the bottle.

Every morning, when she futilely greeted our classmates, she smiled.

When she replied that she "didn't know" why she had attacked Iguchi-san, she grinned.

The night that she first met me in my monstrous form, a satisfied grin.

All those times, there was Yano-san, smiling.

Even on the day when everything changed for our class...

I couldn't breathe.

"What's...wrong? Acchi...kun?"

Her voice felt far away.

I felt myself sinking deeper into my own memories inside my head.

So many, *many* times I had seen that smile. Every time, I had wondered, how could she keep smiling like that?

It was because there was something wrong with her in the head. Because she lived by a different philosophy from the rest of us that she could always smile, I thought; so happily, so freely, despite everything around her.

That was normal, I thought, because she was different from me. Thinking that way helped me understand it. I was glad to think that way.

"Acchi...kun?"

Just then, her alarm went off.

Saved by the bell.

At this juncture there was no point in my even asking what she would have done had the alarm gone off when the others were still here.

"I-I better hurry up and get this cabinet back into the classroom," I said.

Brought back to awareness by the sound of the alarm, I swallowed up the cabinet. Now that I had done it once, the second time was a breeze. After we solemnly put the cabinet back into place, it was time to depart from the darkened school.

"See you...later," she said at the gate, but I could not reply.

I didn't look at her face.

"Thank...you."

I replied simply, "Mm," before leaping off into the night, leaving the place behind.

At first, I thought that I might continue on to somewhere else, but all sorts of unwanted memories began rushing through my head, and instead I found myself following Yano-san, watching over her as she tottered along on her bike.

I remembered her smiling the other day, a smile aimed at no one, when she was all alone.

And then, I came to one more unwanted realization.

Yano-san no longer smiled at me, the monster, like that.

I couldn't come to the school at night anymore.

At Night,
I Become a Monster

Thursday
DAY

IT WAS A MORNING like any other. A normal, unproblematic everyday morning.

I took care not to look at Yano as she entered the classroom, giving her cheerful greeting. I carefully avoided looking her way as she was pelted with eraser shavings and when the other girls said cruel things about her well within earshot. I tried not to look at her and see the face that she always made, that she was probably making now.

What was different today was my own perception, but I should have been able to put that from my mind, so I decided not to pay any more attention to her than usual.

Besides, there were three particular things other than Yano for me to concern myself with. I decided to focus on those.

The first was that Motoda had not come to school. Honestly, as far as he was concerned, it would be more of a mistake for him to show up, given what had happened just last night. No one was likely to believe that he had actually seen a monster. It would be weird for someone to accept such a thing that easily.

The second thing was that no one brought up the problem of the lamp being broken in the middle of the night at all. Perhaps it had been kept a secret so as to squash any strange rumors, but still, it bothered me.

The final thing was that yesterday someone had broken the window of the baseball club room again. Kasai laughed that it was probably Motoda who'd done it, and he hadn't shown today because he was afraid of getting caught, but knowing that this was probably not the case, I began to worry that the culprit might have seen me in my kaiju form.

I wasn't interested in scaring intruders away from the school again. Besides, I wouldn't be coming back here at night anymore.

During the twenty-minute break after second period, I decided to go and take a look at the broken lamp.

I slipped out of the classroom, pretending that I was headed for the bathroom. As I thought about it, it had probably already been fixed anyway, but I still wanted to see for myself. Of course, I probably only became concerned about the light because I wanted an excuse to leave the classroom—just as Motoda had made up a pretext for sneaking into the school.

When I climbed to the fourth floor, sure enough, the broken light bulb had been exchanged for an intact one. I continued up to the fifth floor to make sure that no traces of last night's scuffle remained, but there was nothing really to see, so I did my business in the fifth floor bathroom and started back to the classroom.

On the way, I passed by a classmate, about to ascend from the fourth floor. It wasn't great that someone had seen me descending from the fifth, but given who it was, it was probably no big deal.

I casually raised a hand and greeted her.

"Yo. Off to the library?"

"Mm," Midorikawa replied, nodding in such a way that implied I shouldn't ask questions that I already knew the answers to. Still, I thought that I might try making a bit of conversation.

I do realize that this was just another excuse to keep away from the classroom for as long as possible.

"What're you reading?" I asked.

She held the book in her hands out to me. This was an appropriately meaningless thing to ask, so I was surprised when I took a closer look at the cover.

"Harry Potter."

"Mm."

"...Are the books good, too?" I asked.

"Mm."

I was a bit relieved to see her nod. It was an utterly meaningless relief. It occurred to me that the conversation was now over, and that not only was Midorikawa unlikely to offer up any new topics, but I wasted more than enough time. She looked towards the stairs that stretched up to the fifth floor.

"O-oh, yeah, I just wanted to fix my bedhead a bit, someplace where nobody else could see."

A reasonable excuse. Midorikawa replied, "Mm," with a nod. What was that affirmation in response to? Did she mean it like,

Oh yeah, yeah, sure, of course that's your excuse, whatever? Kasai would be totally disillusioned, if that was the case.

Now that I was already drawing out the conversation, I decided to try and promote my friend a little bit.

"Oh yeah, by the way, you hear that someone broke the baseball club's window again?"

"Mm."

"Oh, so you did know. There's a lot of destructive things happening lately, like with Takao's bike."

"Mm."

"And someone messed with Nakagawa's shoes—everyone's all upset thinking it might've been Yano, but even Kasai, who usually doesn't think much about anything, was saying that we don't even have any proof of that, so we probably shouldn't leap to any conclusions..."

Midorikawa said nothing, but she did not tilt her head at this. Maybe I had come on a little too strong with the point I was trying to make. It was impossible to tell from her reaction how she had taken it.

It was probably best to leave it there.

"W-well, I'll see you in class, then."

I stepped past her, taking two, three steps down the stairs, when suddenly I heard, "Kasai-kun is a bad guy."

At first, I had no idea who had spoken to me. As I turned around, I finally remembered the voice as Midorikawa's. For a moment, she locked eyes with me and then turned back and headed for the library.

It had been ages since I had heard her say anything at all outside of class.

Kasai was a bad guy? What?

I watched her disappear around the corner, having no idea what she meant. I thought long and hard about what she was trying to tell me for the rest of the day, but I came to no conclusion. I came up with a lot of hypotheticals, but it wasn't good to dwell on such impossible things.

As far as outstanding incidents were concerned, that was the only one that day.

Well, maybe two—there was still no Totoro key chain hanging from Iguchi's bag.

At Night,
I Become a Monster

Thursday NIGHT

THE WIND ALWAYS felt nice up on the rooftop.

Here I was, I thought, despite saying that I wouldn't come. I was up on the rooftop tonight because I could not put aside the one-in-a-million chance that Motoda and his friends might be stupid enough to return.

I confirmed that Yano-san was in the classroom and then left a clone standing outside the front door. I myself had no intention of meeting up with her.

Unlike yesterday, the school was quiet tonight. I turned my face into the night wind, letting all manner of thoughts run through my mind.

Why had Midorikawa said those words to me?

She had been reading Harry Potter. I genuinely wanted to ask her what she thought about it.

What was with Kasai?

The baseball club's window was broken again...

Perhaps the reason that those guys knew that the classroom door would be unlocked when I was chasing them was because they had already been inside once.

Maybe Yano-san knew that, which was why she was hiding in the supply cabinet. If that were the case, then she was far too careless in giving a reply. Stupid, even.

...Hang on.

...

She...was scared...?

No matter what I thought about, my thoughts all led me to the same point.

I had felt my own fear when I heard Yano-san's words, although it was a different type of fear than hers. I worried that, having heard those words, my attitude towards her was going to veer away from the rest of the class. If my thinking was aberrant, if my judgement was impaired, then who knew when I might suddenly slip up and do the wrong thing, say the wrong thing.

I could not allow myself to slip up like Iguchi-san and see my daily life ruined. I could think of nothing worse.

I ground my monstrous teeth in resolve.

Which type are you? I thought I heard her voice echo.

Well, I certainly wasn't a Yano-san type.

Finally, midnight break drew to an end. Just as Yano-san opened the classroom door, I dismissed my clone.

Regardless of my presence—or lack thereof—Yano-san had her fill of midnight break and then headed home. I realized that, without my noticing, the midnight hour had become the focus of my nights.

Somehow, that felt dreadful. I decided to spend the rest of the night traveling here and there for sport.

No one knew that I was there.

At Night,
I Become a Monster

Friday
DAY

*I*BARELY GOT a full five minutes' reprieve. A joy filled my
heart after meeting up with Kudou around the shoe boxes and
seeing her double-toothed smile, but it quickly withered away.

"Good...morning."

As Kudou and I headed to the classroom together, Yano came
down the stairs and gave us her usual cheerful greeting. As always,
I ignored her. I didn't look at her face. Kudou, naturally, ignored
her as well. That was our class's way, after all. Yano, likewise, continued straight down the stairs, not seeking any reply.

Just as the interaction ended, and I began to feel relieved,
Kudou turned towards the descending Yano and threw the iced
coffee carton she was holding at her—or so it appeared. I only
turned to look after hearing the high sound of a shoe squeaking
across the floor, so I could only guess how Kudou had moved, but
I'm pretty sure I was on the mark.

The carton struck Yano in the back of the head and then fell to the floor. It seemed to be nearly empty, but a bit of coffee still spurted from the straw out onto Yano's hair.

"Ow."

Hearing this from Yano, Kudou turned right back around, grinning at me, and then picked the conversation right back up where she had left it with a "So, anyway..."

That was dangerous. Still, I managed to force my body back into its original course of action, matching pace with Kudou with an "Uh-huh." In other words, I probably corrected course into someone who had met up with a classmate and was now walking to the classroom with them side by side, listening to their gossip.

As we arrived at the classroom and I reconsidered this accomplishment, realizing what it meant, a shiver ran down my spine.

Could it be that I was already beginning to veer off the rails?

Kudou used to be someone who ignored Yano so effortlessly, one wondered if she truly even really saw her. The only times she ever actively joined in on the harassment were when someone else cajoled her into it or when Yano overstepped the bounds of Kudou's personal space. I had assumed her opinions and attitude to be the median amongst our classmates when it came to Yano.

And yet now she had done this thing.

Perhaps the incidents with Iguchi and Nakagawa had raised the bar for our class's acceptable behavior, increased the demands of our shared sense of unity.

I corrected my stance.

I needed to be careful and decide how I was going to act. If I let myself slip, I might soon find myself targeted as an outsider. As I fretted over this, someone who lived life at his own pace approached, someone who never had such worries.

"You think that kaiju ate Motoda's soul or somethin'? Ahaha."

Kasai's cheerful laughter was a balm.

I know that he meant it only as a joke, but as I thought about it, I realized that he was fairly on the mark. If Motoda refused to come to school because of what I had done to him, then one might as well say that I *had* eaten his soul.

Kasai took out his phone and showed me photos of a stray cat he had come across the day before. It was the same stray I had seen at night.

If the issue of cats versus dogs ever came up, Kasai was most assuredly a cat person, so I fell in step with that, talking to him just as another cat person would. Suddenly, however, a large shadow fell over us from the hallway.

"Kasai, hand it over."

It was the homeroom teacher of Class 4. Kasai sputtered, "Wha?! Seriously?!" He didn't recoil at all, even in the face of such an imposing authority figure. Around the room, a number of students suddenly shoved their hands into their pockets or their desks.

"Yes, seriously."

"This is important to me, though! I should get to take care of it myself!"

"Then you should have left it at home instead of bringing it to school. C'mon, give it over, now."

Reluctantly, Kasai placed his phone into the teacher's out-stretched hand, and with that the teacher left, saying that he would hand it over to our homeroom teacher. Seemingly utterly mortified, Kasai moaned, "Seriously, though? Everyone's got 'em, even Nakagawa..." He petitioned the sympathies of those around him, drawing piteous looks.

As I watched Kasai head to his seat, still peeved, I finally understood something that had been bothering me for some time.

Ah, I see. So that's why Iguchi's Totoro key chain was missing from her bag.

It was something that was important to her, and it was something that she could no longer hope to protect all on her own.

I glanced over at Iguchi. She was nodding and grinning at something the other girls were saying. Though they had made tenuous amends, Iguchi was well aware that she now stood on the wrong side of our bubble of shared unity. I wonder if she was scared, too...

I quickly put aside the thought. But now that I knew the reason for Iguchi's actions, it made sense that I never saw Yano playing with her phone during the day, the way that she always did at night.

She knew firsthand how much devastation could be caused by harming something that was precious to someone else.

Just then, Midorikawa came into the room, a library book in hand.

"Morning."

"Mm."

Naturally, she gave no further reply.

Now and then I thought about Midorikawa, the only one in our class who was permitted to go against the grain. I couldn't envy her. One step in the wrong direction and she would end up in the same place as Yano. She had only ended up in a defensible position because she knew the right expressions to make, because she never showed fear. However, one of these days, she might just slip from that pedestal of hers.

It was perhaps because Midorikawa knew this that she made such a show of bringing in a book from the library every day. *Oh, poor me*, this routine seemed to say, *I'm so afraid of bringing my own books now that I have to leave them at home.* If it really was a ploy of hers, then it had proved almost disgustingly successful.

The bell rang, and our homeroom teacher arrived. Just as he was in the midst of informing Kasai that he should come to the staff room after school, Yano dragged her feet into the room. "Be in your seat before the bell," he sighed in warning, to which Yano replied, "O...kay," and took her seat.

Normally, he would not have bothered about her any further; it was like he'd given up on worrying about Yano's attitude. Today was different.

"Look here, what would you have done if today was exam day? Do you really think you could just say 'Okay' and be done with it?"

While I wished to retort that of course she would be more careful on an exam day, the thought simultaneously occurred to me that Yano would probably come in just as late no matter how important the day was.

"Oi. Yano."

Just as I sighed internally over how pointless this sermon was, an angry voice rang out elsewhere in the room.

"This is nothing to smile about!"

I felt a wave ripple through my body, the very same kind that I did during the night.

Then the teacher really laid into a sermon. At first, it was directed specifically at Yano, but at length it blossomed into a tirade concerning the entire class, including addressing Kasai's phone, self-discipline, our duties to society, and such and so forth, eating up all of our time and dragging on and on until just before the bell that signaled the break before first period.

It began in a gloomy atmosphere. The atmosphere could be nothing *but* gloomy. Everyone's irritation was so palpable you could practically feel it press against your skin. It didn't take long for that same feeling of resentment to be redirected toward the person who was at the root of it all.

At this point, I don't think I need to explain any further.

Friday
NIGHT

THE NIGHT PASSED much like the one before.
Besides my own feelings, all was quiet.

At Night,
I Become a Monster

Monday
DAY

$\mathcal{E}$VER SINCE I BECAME a monster, I had stopped sleeping.

Thus, the form that my body took was determined by the boundary between day and night. Typically, I returned to my human form between four and five A.M., around when the sun began to rise. Naturally, when I returned home in monster form, not a soul was awake in my house. There was a long stretch until breakfast and heading to school, so I had a fair amount of free time.

A number of times, I had decided that I might at least try to sleep, even if only for an hour or two, and gone to snuggle in beneath my futon. However, again and again as I lay there, not sleeping, the smell of coffee would eventually come wafting up from the first floor. Ultimately, I gave up on it.

Today, as usual, I sat alone in my room on my bed with too much time on my hands. If I turned on my lights and the glow seeped out into the hallway, my family might notice and say something, so I opened my curtains and sat there quietly in the dark. It had been overcast since Saturday, and the moon was hidden.

Previously, I would use the faint light from my cell phone screen to read manga by, but lately I had no interest in this. Instead, once I finished my homework, I would just sit there blankly, like a fixture, waiting for time to tick by on its own.

As long as I thought about nothing, this time was rather relaxing. Actually trying to keep my mind clear was rather less so. The gurus in movies had the power to totally clear their mind, but even they often said something like: true zen takes much training.

I lay sprawled on my bed, gazing upward. Though I could not sleep, as long as I stared up at the ceiling, it felt like my body was resting.

If I was going to be thinking about things anyway, they may as well be fun things. I put my hands on my head and started to imagine what I'd do the following night.

When night fell, I would probably head to the school and watch over Yano from the shadows, as always, and then I would be free to go pass the time elsewhere. So what would I do tonight? I imagined various destinations, all sorts of ways to spend the hours. I had visited a number of islands over the weekend. When I crossed over the waves, I found nature and people who I had likely never once crossed paths with before. There were plenty of animals beyond the usual cats and dogs, too, but they all fled as soon as they became aware of my presence.

Maybe it was time to try sightseeing in another country. I supposed that, though I couldn't stay long, I could make it to some of the other countries of Asia, at the very least. And if that worked, then the whole world was my oyster.

As I pondered this, suddenly, a thought occurred to me.

Just how long did I intend to keep doing this? I'd been thinking as though these strange nights of mine would last forever, but in truth, I had no idea how long the nightly transformations might continue. Like I'd thought on the night I chased Motoda away, my nights might return to normal at any moment.

I prayed that it would continue for as long as possible. But what did "as long as possible" mean? Until the end of junior high? Until the end of high school? Until the end of university? Until I was an old man?

I couldn't really pin it down in concrete terms. At the very least, it would be nice if it lasted until I had some freedom. Until I didn't feel so stifled all the time. I'd love to keep my monstrous form at my disposal until then.

And still, just when would *that* be?

Perhaps it was like Noto said—you could live a bit more freely once you're an adult.

If that was true, at what age did she mean? How many more years would it take?

How much longer would I have to keep watch to ensure that no one ruined my classmate's nights? How much longer would Yano keep up this habit of sneaking into the school at night?

How long would this go on? I don't simply mean protecting her midnight breaks. How much longer would Yano keep irritating us all by being unable to read the room? How long would

Midorikawa refuse to communicate with others? How long would Motoda and Nakagawa take pleasure in harming others? How long would Iguchi be unable to have faith in the people around her?

Just how long would it all continue?

Perhaps it might end once we graduated from junior high. Perhaps we would all go off to different high schools, our class becoming only a thing of memory, and everyone's treatment of one another—their personalities, their beliefs, their twisted hobbies—would all change.

But who could know for sure?

Once again, I felt anger build up inside of me at Noto for saying something so clueless.

Then I realized that this was no time for me to be worrying about other people. I needed to keep from slipping up in the classroom, to take care not to step out of line, to live my life with the utmost caution in the upcoming week. As I imagined this, I felt a cold sweat come over me.

It was fine, though. I still had the night.

As I comforted myself, shifting from side to side, the sounds of human life began to stir.

There was a light shower coming down on the way to school—a gloomy Monday, through and through. I walked with my umbrella out, cursing the weather that I hoped might suddenly clear up overnight.

I continued along the road, thinking over the day's schedule. There would be an extended homeroom, then English, then math. Not an especially taxing day. The issue here was how much of the class's tension from last Friday had carried over into this week. I had to be extra careful when gauging it. If I didn't, I might find myself suddenly on the wrong side at any time. I might end up outside of the circle of unity before I knew it. Like day and night, my position could be reversed in an instant. And just as drastically as between human and monster, I would change.

I had to choose my actions wisely. Truthfully, even the sort of things I had been thinking about at dawn were starting to veer off course, so perhaps it was already too late.

I had to be careful.

"Acchi!"

As someone called me, I returned to my senses. I turned around to see a jovial Kasai.

"Ahaha, you're totally soaked."

Apparently, I had neglected to properly keep the rain off of me while I was spacing out. I brushed off my dampened left shoulder and corrected my stance—both bodily and mentally.

"Don't usually see you walking, Acchi."

"No? I always walk when it's raining."

"Huh. Guess so."

Kasai lived comparatively close to the school and always walked in the mornings. After school, he often hitched a ride home on the back of someone's bike. Obviously, such a thing was prohibited within the schoolgrounds, but as soon as he stepped outside the gates, such rules probably meant nothing to him.

Little of note happened as we walked along, avoiding puddles. The usual group who were chauffeured by their parents on rainy days passed us by, and eventually, we arrived safely at the school gates. *"Safely,"* I thought internally and then had to laugh at myself for thinking something so carefree.

It was here that the real trial would begin. To put it in a word, the path stretching forward from here was a minefield.

Kasai flew through the gates, not a care in the world, striding nimbly around every single land mine as he headed towards the entrance. As skilled as always, that one.

I could do no such thing. I didn't have the slightest bit of innate sense that allowed Kasai to live that way. I had to proceed step by cautious step through life, careful not to step on any of the mines, but making sure that that vigilance did not weigh me down. If not, I would end up exposed. Shunned.

But the tedium of this slow progress weighed on me. It was my own fault, a flaw in my disposition. And yet, there were times when I worried I might have this problem forever, just as I had at dawn.

I shook my head, as though shaking off the raindrops from my hair, shedding myself of these cowardly thoughts as I did.

I just had to keep living carefully. I just had to be sure to always choose the right things. It wasn't that complicated.

As I politely folded my umbrella outside of the entrance, careful not to send the drops flying onto anyone's uniform, I heard a cheerful voice.

"Heya, Non-chan, you goin' out?"

"My name is not *Non-chan*."

I tapped my umbrella along the ground, drawing closer to the little scene playing out between Kasai and Noto in front of our class's shoe boxes. I noticed that Noto was holding her shoes and umbrella, currently donning said shoes. She had probably just come from the nurse's office.

"Morning, Adachi-kun."

"G'mornin'."

"One of the first-years fell off of their bike and broke a bone, so I have to take them to the hospital."

"You can't just leave 'em?"

"Kasai, would you want me to leave you to fend for yourself if you broke a bone? There will be someone else in charge while I'm gone. You boys do your best in class today."

With that, Noto hurried out of the entryway.

"I guess that's just another of a school nurse's duties," said Kasai, laughing nonchalantly as he watched her walk away. "Still, seems like she's got it pretty easy. It's not like she's gotta do all that much."

Being a school nurse did seem pretty easy...from what we had seen firsthand, anyway.

But really, there was no reason to even consider anything more than that. Having the ability to imagine things beyond what you could see with your own two eyes was fruitless, excessive. Kasai knew this well enough. We switched from our sneakers into our indoor shoes, and finally, it was the start to another perfectly typical week.

I neither enjoyed nor particularly hated the fact that things were just as they always were. It was just that, even on days like these that weren't especially bad, I still had to take care that my comfortable existence remained intact.

Honestly, I didn't really need to be thinking about any of this. Once I was an adult, I would be free. I just had to live a proper life. That took even less work than avoiding traffic accidents. All I had to worry about was just avoiding the things that I shouldn't do. There was no point in wondering now how long things might continue.

All that I had to maintain here was my place. I could come to school normally, sit for my lessons, and take my breaks. I just had to be sure that this tolerable status quo didn't suddenly take a turn for the worse. I needed to keep on maintaining things as I had thus far, keep on with the strategies that had gotten me to where I was.

I, the human, could accomplish at least that much.

When I was a monster, though, things were different. With my imagination at my fingertips, I no longer had to focus so intensely on myself.

It was the same as always. As long as I could preserve the status quo, everything would be fine.

As long as I could keep doing the right thing, as I always had.

I settled my resolve and straightened my back. I ascended the stairs alongside Kasai, walked down the hall, and stepped into the classroom.

It was then that it happened.

Something landed at my feet.

I don't know what course of events lead to this, or what was going on, or why this thing had ended up just at my feet. At this juncture, I had no idea what the item might be. All I knew was that, besides Kasai, the eyes of everyone in the classroom were on the thing that had landed at my feet, and on me.

Wondering just what it was, I glanced at the bulging white paper bag at my feet. There was something written on it. I took in the warped lettering.

Yano Satsuki.

It was Yano's.

This was the moment of truth.

All of the things I had been thinking about since dawn spilled over in my mind, and amongst those thoughts was a spot that went pitch-black. From out of that darkness a dim thought of Iguchi drifted out. Actually, it wasn't Iguchi. It was something far more terrifying—the thought of Iguchi's harassment.

Here I was again, at the mercy of Murphy's law.

I looked once again at the faces of everyone in the classroom. Everyone there was scrutinizing my actions. Amongst them was Yano, rushing my way with an "Oh!"

A shiver ran down my spine.

I had to do the right thing.

There would be no making the excuse that I wasn't thinking. Being careful meant one could never leave these sort of things to chance.

I reconfirmed what lay at my feet. Though it was not for long, I thought hard, made my decision, and acted.

With my right foot, I stomped down on the white paper bag. The thing inside made a crunching sound.

It was as though that sound was the key that undid the spell. With that single step of mine, time began to move in the classroom once more. Everyone turned their gazes away from me and returned to what they were doing.

I felt relief. That sound had cleared up any doubts I had about myself. I had done the right thing as a member of this class. With that fateful stomp as my first step, I continued straight on to my desk.

I knew at once that, normally, such an action would see me criticized, but that was the right thing to do, here in this room. I had merely evaluated my options and properly aligned myself with the views of my classmates. Yes, that was what I told myself.

As I set my bag on my desk, desperately trying to steady my racing heartbeat, Kudou jabbed me in the side. At first, I was afraid that she was going to reprimand me, but instead there was a lively grin upon her face.

Even Kudou should have known how wicked a thing it was to step on something belonging to someone else. Not just Kudou— that should have been common sense for everyone in the room. And yet, here was Kudou smiling, not a single one of my class- mates looking to rebuke me for it, because what I had done was the right thing to do, only now, only here. I had succeeded by the barometer of how much ill-will or anger one should show towards Yano, by the strange metric this class used to judge one another. That test was sacred within these walls.

And I knew that. And yet, my heart kept beating faster and faster, because I could not find solace in the shelter of our class's unique mindset. I should have recognized how important this was, but facts that only I—that only I and Yano— knew, kept me from feeling that righteousness.

The heat within my body rose as a war waged within my own heart.

If such a thing would have been allowed, I would have done anything to question Yano at once.

Why?

Why hadn't she left something important to her at home? Why would she bring it to school during the day? In my moment of panic, I hadn't even thought to hesitate, not knowing what was inside that bulging white bag. But I should have at least known what it was for.

And yet, I had stepped on it.

"Oh," said Yano, picking up the bag, before peeking inside. "It's...broken," she muttered, trudging to the back of the classroom and shutting it inside of her locker. I watched as she did this, still sitting next to a gleeful Kudou.

There was no need to even set my powers of imagination to work. I had known the answer just from looking at that bag. I did not need to imagine it at all.

For the first time ever, true guilt panged within my heart. The guilt filled me like a balloon until I was ready to burst.

After all, I had seen in the wake of my own footstep one other warped line of letters on that white bag, below Yano's name.

To: Noto-sensei.

It should be "for," shouldn't it?

Within my heart, I could only repeat that it was none of my business.

Monday
NIGHT

YANO-SAN HAD BROUGHT IT with her during the day because that was the only time she could give it to her.

She had probably brought it all the way to class instead of giving it to her during arrival because she had happened to stop by the nurse's office while Noto-sensei was busy tending to the injured first-year.

Though I had known that it was this week, I had no idea that Noto-sensei's birthday was today.

However, knowing this did nothing to ease my feelings of guilt.

And so, that night, I decided to go and apologize.

I couldn't apologize to her during the day, but I could at least do it at night. I, the monster, could accomplish at least that much.

It was the first time I'd be seeing Yano-san at night in a while. Realizing that it was also the first time that I had ever come for the express purpose of resolving something between us, I began to grow a bit nervous.

It was possible that she might not even come tonight. It was raining, after all. She might be depressed over what I had done to her.

If she was here, it was possible that she might be opposed to my apology. She might say that if it was something worth apologizing for, then I shouldn't had done it in the first place. Even though I had acted correctly as a member of our class, I could not expect Yano-san to accept that.

I was uneasy, but I could deal with any complaints. However, I had no idea what I would do if her reaction was any more violent than that.

I thought of Yano-san's face.

After a slightly more delayed transformation than usual, I flew to the school. With the power of my imagination, I sprouted wings like a giant bat and soared through the sky. *I bet that if Yano-san saw those wings, she would be delighted,* I thought to myself, hoping to absolve my own sin.

As always, when I arrived at school, I alighted upon the roof, remembering the first time that I had come there. This time, however, I didn't feel that same rush that I did then. The only similarity between this time and that one was my own nervousness.

The school, as always, was quiet. Though the building was all shut up for the night, not a single door or window open, it felt far more accessible than it ever did during the day, full of the chatter of students, the warmth of bodies.

It was because I was a monster and because there was no one here right now. When I was a human, I felt closed in. Not by walls or ceilings but by people's sense of justice, their ill intent, and their shared sense of unity.

There was no doubting that Yano-san felt even more trapped, more stifled, than I did.

Of course she would. This empty, open school at night was probably the only place where she could breathe freely.

Suddenly, I felt like for the first time, I truly understood what she meant by "midnight break."

I soon arrived at the front of the classroom, opening the door before I gathered my full resolve. The more prepared I was, the less likely that I would have been able to show my face.

Yano-san was inside the classroom, sitting at her seat, as always. She looked my way and opened her mouth stupidly.

"Whoa, long...time no...see."

There had only been two nights where I hadn't shown up. Four, if you include the weekend, but perhaps Yano-san felt the passage of time a bit differently than I did.

The daytime probably felt very long for her.

"Yeah, been a while."

I moved to the back of the classroom and morphed myself into a comfortable size. As I wondered how to break the ice, Yano-san put her phone into her pocket and turned back towards me.

"So," she said, and I grew uneasy, worried that I was about to be attacked for what I had done during the day. "Have you been any...where fun lately?"

I was wrong.

It was a question, abrupt as always. I nodded, assuming that she was referring to the nighttime.

"I've been a lot of places."

"Really?"

"Nowhere super fun, though. I tried going a bunch of places to sightsee, but there was no one around, and shrines and stuff are super creepy to go to at night."

"It's weird... that you get scared...even when you look like... that."

As always, her choice of words was just a little bit off, I thought. It was the kind of phrasing that invited conflicts and misunderstandings. Still, I was not going to bother saying anything about that today.

"Acchi...kun, do you prefer...Europe or A...sia?"

"What's with those two choices? I've never been outside Japan."

"I see. I...was actually wondering, what would happen if...you went overseas at...night, and it turned to morning because of the... time difference."

"...I wonder about that, too."

I hadn't thought of it before, but her innocent question bothered me.

"It'd probably be bad if you turned...back into your daytime form over...the ocean."

"...That'd be dangerous."

Just this morning at dawn, I had been thinking that I might go overseas. Perhaps it would be best to put those thoughts to rest.

"I wonder if you could ma...nipulate time with your powers of i...magination, Acchi-kun."

"No way. I'm pretty sure I can't control anything outside of myself."

Even with this impossible form of mine, some things were still out of the question.

"I...see."

Her disappointment was easy to read, almost conspicuously so. She looked up at the ceiling and sputtered out a sigh.

"I thought you...could make it nighttime for...ever."

I concealed the chattering of my body.

If only it could be night forever.

That was probably an earnest desire for Yano-san.

Still, that was impossible. No matter what, morning would come, even if for Yano-san the rising of the sun must have felt like standing before the gates of Hell. There was no such thing as an endless night. It pained me that there was no way that I could possibly grant her wish.

"Well, have you tried?" I thought she might ask.

Unfortunately for her, if I really could make the night draw on longer, it would have already happened.

It would have happened even before the first time I encountered her at night. Because I, too, had always thought how nice it would be if the night went on forever. And yet the sun always rose. I returned to my human form, changed my clothes, ate breakfast, and headed to school.

Even I, who did not hate school from the bottom of my heart, had had such thoughts. I understood Yano-san's words, and the fact that they were more than just passing suggestion, so much that it hurt.

How nice it would be, if my powers lent me such ability. Maybe, if I thought harder, harder than I ever had before, I might be able to grant her that eternal night.

"So, what...should we do...to...night?"

Apparently she hadn't noticed how my droplets quivered.

"I mean, I dunno."

Naturally, I hadn't been thinking about such things. I had come here to apologize, after all. But I was still a bit relieved to hear Yano-san's question, to hear her tossing out suggestions as usual, not appearing particularly upset about what happened earlier that day. Maybe she did understand that what I had done was only the logical next step of the things that our classmates had done.

Even so, I still couldn't think of a way to broach that conversation.

"The baseball club's window isn't even broken anymore," I said.

"They probably couldn't keep up with it any...more."

"Keep up with what?"

"Let's...go to the...gym."

Yano-san completely ignoring my question raised my hopes. The same as always. She was the same as always.

It might be nice to go to the gym. It was a more open space, and in a less serious atmosphere. It might be easier for me to apologize, and there would be plenty of things there to pass the time.

I decided to go along with her suggestion.

"Acchi...kun, you don't really have any...opinions, do you?"

"I mean, there's just nowhere that I really want to go in the school at night."

"Oh, I...see."

Her observation might have actually contained a deeper dig at my own character, I thought momentarily, but I felt sure that I was overthinking it.

I had Yano-san exit the room first and then locked the door. "That's so han...dy," said Yano-san as she watched me dispatch a clone to run ahead, though she had already seen me do that plenty of times before.

We descended the stairs and headed for the gym. Yano-san's footsteps were as noisy as ever, but I didn't scold her for it. We passed by the changing rooms and by the place where I had kicked her. Beyond the passageway, the door to the gymnasium was firmly shut.

Yano-san waited by the door while I slipped inside.

I returned from my liquid-like state back into my full monster form. The interior of the gym was like being sealed away in an airtight prison. Amidst the piercing silence, it was as though I could hear the echoes of all of the sounds generated by the classes and club practices during the day, shut up in here with me.

Suddenly growing fearfully aware of the fact that I was literally shut inside, I quickly opened the door with my tail. Without so much as a word of thanks, Yano-san, who was still waiting patiently, shed her shoes and stepped into the gym. She took in a deep breath, an almost calculated motion.

"It feels like...there's a lot of sounds in...here."

Seriously? That's what she picked up on by doing that? Not the smell? Then again, I couldn't say anything, since I had thought the exact same thing.

As I closed the door again with my tail, she let out a big noise. "Whoooa. It's su...per dark in...here."

"Yeah."

The emergency lights were on, of course, but in a space as large as the gym, that amount of light wasn't enough for the human eye to rely on.

"Hang on a minute," I said.

I leapt up to the upper floor, leaving Yano-san standing there as I opened up all of the curtains on the high windows with my tail and turned on one row of lights. That should have been enough for Yano-san, the human, to see as well as I could. I prayed that it would not be so much that anyone outside would notice.

By the time I returned, Yano-san had run over to the wall and begun walking along the perimeter of the gym. I changed myself to my comfortable resting size.

Unlike me, the tiny Yano-san had a tiny stride as well, so walking the full length took her some time, after which she returned to me. As she returned, she pointed up at the ceiling.

"Hey... Acchi-kun, go get...that."

I looked up, but at first did not understand what she was indicating. All that I saw when I looked where she was pointing was the ceiling.

"The...ball."

I finally noticed it once she pointed it out. My perception wasn't all that great.

After pondering for a moment what to do, I moved away from Yano-san and unfurled my wings. Just as I had imagined, I heard Yano-san's awed voice behind me as I rose into the air. I could have simply jumped up there, but it was worth bothering to do it this way.

I nudged the basketball that was trapped in the scaffolding until it fell, catching it midway, to keep it from hitting her in the face. I circled the gym as I landed.

I gently chucked the ball in the direction of the arrhythmic applause I received, and it plunked perfectly into the space between Yano-san's hands, mid-clap.

She bounced the ball once against the ground, again not extending any thanks. The ball sprang up in the wrong direction, as though she had not even thought to adjust her power or angle, and then rolled towards me. I grabbed it with my tail and tossed it back. The ball missed her, soaring past, and Yano-san trotted off after it.

For a brief while, she clumsily practiced dribbling, throwing some free throws that fell well short of the basket. Eventually, growing either tired or frustrated, she walked my way and flung the ball at me. What was with that, all of a sudden?

This time, when I caught the ball with my tail and threw it back, she caught it properly and then threw it again my way. Apparently, she had decided we were going to kill time playing catch now. I could go for at least that much.

As the ball went back and forth, back and forth, sailing behind Yano-san countless times, the sound of rain upon the roof grew stronger and stronger. We might have been shut up inside of here, but at least we were protected.

"It's lucky for this little one that you were...here, Acchi...kun," she said, abruptly as ever.

Little one?

"You mean the ball?"

"Yeah. Now we...get to see it living pro...perly, as a ball."

"It's not alive, though."

"It might...be alive, just very quiet."

"That's creepy. We're throwing it around."

Conversation and a game of catch. I realized then that, somehow, somewhere during all this, I had started having fun.

"Isn't there some...thing like that in...the world of Harry... Potter?"

"Well, the pictures and broomsticks talk and move around and stuff, so kind of."

"I see, so...then don't be...so stupid."

"What?"

"Though I guess...we should still be care...ful."

"What are you talking about?"

"So, Acchi...kun."

As always, she wasn't listening to a word I said. With how poor her control of her whole body was, as she took form to throw the ball again, the intonation of her voice was even stranger than usual.

"Mm?"

"Your night...form or your day form... Which is...the real one?"

Perhaps it was because she had thrown the ball with more vigor than before, but it went sailing over my head. The echo of its heavy impact against the wall behind me made my black droplets shiver.

"Huh?"

"Go get the...ball," she said casually, pointing right at me. I obeyed, turning around and picking up the ball behind me with my tail.

"Throw...it."

I threw the ball in an arc. Yano-san deftly caught it.

"Are you a human? Or are you...what you are...now?"

"No, I, uh..."

"I've been wonder...ing which it...is."

This time she flung only words at me, the ball still in her hands.

"Which one...is the real one?"

What exactly was she referring to?

"You know... I..."

Though I hadn't asked her, as per usual, she began speaking about herself.

"I'm not...either one. Day, night, there's...no difference to me. I don't change...at all. Everything around me changes. The time and...the people and things and at...mosphere around me change, but I am...the same, day or night. The dif...ferences mean nothing to...me."

I was lost for words.

"But you, Acchi...kun. You change...completely...between day and night."

What was she talking about?

"So I wonder which...one it is."

She kept pointing straight at me, as though interrogating me.

"I've been thinking about this while you weren't...around," she playfully jabbed.

My black droplets began to quiver, quietly, under the aim of her pointing finger. She was staring straight at me, not averting her eyes.

"I want to...know."

I drew in a single breath.

I doubted that Yano-san was all that strong or all that wise. She probably had simply developed some sort of curiosity. My human form and my monster form—which one was the real one? She had asked me something like this before, about whether I had been born in my monster form. So it made more sense to assume that this was merely an innocent question.

Regardless, to me it seemed as though her teasing was merely a means to hide her true feelings. Hiding the truth behind a different expression, just as Nakagawa-san had when Kasai criticized her.

Maybe it was merely my feelings of guilt at work, but it felt as though I was being reproached. It seemed like she was concealing her anger towards me—for what I had done while a human, naturally.

She hid this to protect herself. To protect the time that she had now, as Iguchi-san and Nakagawa-san had. If she were to grow angry, then the night would be ruined. If she were to grow angry, then the connection that the two of us shared might be severed. It was for this reason, I believed, that she suppressed her feelings and tried to reach an emotional compromise, by eliciting a response from me that she could accept.

I have no idea if my reasoning was correct. I had no idea how to answer her question in a way that she would find acceptable.

Not knowing this, I sidestepped it.

"I'm sorry."

I couldn't answer her question. Instead, I spat out the answer she was truly seeking, flying directly past her inquiry. It was a bit of an evasion, but honestly, it got to the point of what we both had originally been circling around. I felt this was far more meaningful than offering a reply that suited the question that Yano-san had asked, the one which concealed her true feelings. Thus, the deep question that she had asked me was quite convenient for my purposes, if I could speak the truth here now.

"For...what?" she asked, tilting her head theatrically as she rolled the ball between her fingertips.

Of course, she wanted a more concrete apology, I thought.

Normally, that kind of manipulation would have gotten my monstrous hackles up, but for today, at least, she was right to feel as she did. It was natural that she would be angry with me after what I had done.

However, apologizing felt less natural. It was not something that I could do during the day. And so, I stood up straight, bowing down my large, monstrous head towards her.

"I'm sorry."

"O...kay?"

She was acting even more bewildered. Her eyes were big and round, like a child's. Goggling at me as she was, she looked almost stupid.

"Um..."

I began to speak and then closed my mouth. Where had my courage gone?

Hardly ever in my life had I done something with ill intent. Even fewer times had I needed to apologize to someone for doing so. Most rarely of all had I been the sole perpetrator of the act.

All the more reason then, that I should apologize.

It was bad, after all.

Bad.

Bad?

Which was bad?

"About today..." I said and then trailed off.

Which was *worse?*

The thing that I had done today? Or what I did day in and day out?

The explicit bullying? Or the implicit?

Motoda and Nakagawa-san, or me?

Yano-san or the rest of us?

"I'm sorry for stepping on your present for Noto-sensei."

So many other words, other questions ran through my head, but I offered her the words I had already prepared as they were, not second-guessing them. If I let myself overthink it, I would never say anything at all.

So, it was good that I was able to say it. Still, between my nerves and everything else, I had to avert my eyes. Realizing, however, that this made my apology seem like a lie, I looked her properly in the face.

I saw it.

I took in the transformation of her face as she accepted my apology, clearly, with my own eight eyes.

Her lips twitched.

Yano-san...

"Don't a...pologize for things that...happen during the...day."

...did not grin at me.

Her lips still pursed, the reply she gave me was one that I had heard before.

Honestly, I had suspected that she might say such a thing, a prediction which turned out correct. So, that was all right. The words, anyway.

What I had feared most was not her words, but her expression. I didn't know what I would do if I saw that face; that face that only I understood the meaning of, that face that she showed towards those terrible people.

In the end, however, she had not made that face.

So, that should have been just fine too, and yet...

"You aren't...going to smile?" For some reason, these needless words came spilling from my jagged mouth.

"Hm...hmm?"

"Even after what I did?"

There was no reason for me to ask her such a question, no reason for me to put my own head on the chopping block in that way, but even a monster like me could not take back words I had already spoken.

Yano-san's eyes opened wide. She clapped her hands theatrically, saying, "Oh."

And then, she smiled. It was a peculiar smile.

But...not a smug one. It was a real, natural smile.

"Acchi-kun, I'm not...afraid of you."

"Why not?"

There went my mouth, all on its own.

"Why not? Even after what I did to you?" I asked.

My voice reverberated curiously throughout the cavernous gym. The trapped sounds and smells from the daytime all seemed to vanish.

"*Why?*"

Yano-san tilted her head, curiously.

Even I had no idea why I had asked this question.

"Be...cause..." she said, "You look at...me, Acchi-kun."

I had asked this without a hint of sincerity. And yet, she had answered me straight-on.

However, I did not understand the meaning of this reply. I truly did not understand.

"Did you act...ually *want* me..."

Her words that followed rumbled through me like thunder.

"...to be afraid of you, Acchi...kun?"

...Ah.

"That's...weird."

She bounced the ball once. This time, it returned properly to her fingertips. The sound of the ball striking the floor seemed to tear through the very membrane of my heart.

Then I realized.

All of the true feelings that had been trapped inside that membrane came pouring into my brain at once, and my body went numb with realization.

Oh. *Oh.* I see.

I could not answer her question.

It was not as though all the words had vanished from my head; it was that the true answer to her question was something that I could never allow anyone to see. As I listened to her, I finally realized that all this time I had been mistaking the name of the thing that I had kept concealed inside my heart.

I could not believe this revelation, but I no longer had the means to dismiss it.

In the place within my heart that I thought held guilt, I ached, as though pierced by a needle.

It was Yano-san's words that had pierced me.

Right on the mark.

"Acchi...kun, *you're* the weird one."

"..."

"Just returning a...little something you...said to me on the rooftop, hee hee."

I wanted her to be afraid of me. Just as she had said.

The reason for this was simple. If she were afraid, then I wouldn't have to worry about her anymore. I wanted her to fear me, to hate me, to think that I was an awful person. It would be so much easier if she could just cast me aside, wouldn't it? For her to rebuke me, to deny me, even after I had wholeheartedly apologized. That would be so much simpler. I'm sure I had believed that.

I couldn't say that I didn't still feel that way.

I was afraid that she would continue seeking my aid. I had so carelessly, readily, come here to apologize, had I not?

Surely, there was some part of me that was still convinced that what I had done today was right.

The name of that tarnished spot I had found within my soul... I don't believe that its name was truly "guilt."

"Oh...or..."

Surely not knowing the darkness of my heart, she pointed at me, her neck crooked strangely. "Are you...afraid of your...self, Acchi-kun?"

"...Huh?"

"It's o...kay, don't be a...fraid," she said, in a *Nausicaa*-like quote, grinning not smugly but flippantly. When I didn't reply, however, she tilted her head the other way and asked again, "Am I wrong?"

I said nothing.

"Well...then, could it...be..."

She pointed now not at me, but at herself.

"You're a...fraid of... me?"

Out of the whole rapid-fire volley of her questions, that was the only one I could nod in reply to.

With my simple nod, a sour look came naturally over her face. She recoiled, a perfectly normal reaction.

"But...why? I haven't done anything bad to...you."

No, she hadn't. She was awkward, and strange, and slow on the uptake, but she had done nothing cruel to me. What I feared about her was not as pure and simple a reason as that.

"...Because I don't understand," I said.

"Under...stand what?"

I believe I was trying to feign innocence here, craftily showing her only what could readily be seen on my sleeve, not wanting her to see the true darkness inside of me.

Still, I told her the truth, the truth I always carried.

"Because you're so different from me that I don't understand what you're thinking."

So there's no point in even worrying about this, I wanted to say.

"Huh? But isn't it...normal to be...different?"

She didn't sound as though she was belittling me.

"To not know...what someone else is...thin...king?"

Yano-san furrowed her brow, as though *she* did not understand what I was saying or thinking at all. That was the face—the face I was afraid of. The face where she didn't try at all to conceal her lack of comprehension.

"In that case, then...who do you stand with, Acchi...kun?"

Who? Various faces passed through my mind. She held her hand out in front of her face and bent her thumb.

"The in...secure, useless...girl who doesn't ac...tually look down on anyone but still pretends she...enjoys bullying?"

Who was she talking about?

Then she bent her forefinger.

"The smart...boy who's always play...ing around, who al...ways knows how to...act, what the people around him will...do?"

Who was she talking about?

Then she bent her middle finger.

"Our stupid classmates who feel res...ponsible for taking revenge on be...half of someone who got into a fight and had something...ter...rible done to them by a former friend and...can't bother making up with them, only ever nodding at every...one?"

Just who the hell was she talking about?

Finally, she bent her ring and pinky finger down together and squeezed them all tight, pointing that fist at me.

"Me, you...and all of them, we're...all different. It's normal to be...different. So there's...no reason why you should understand what I'm...thinking."

"..."

"And even...so, you're afraid of...*me*?"

This time, I could not nod. What she said was completely off the mark of what I had tried to convey. At the same time, part of me thought that maybe what she said *was* true.

As I puzzled over this, her expression changed.

Her eyebrows lowered, and the corners of her mouth rose, just a little. It was not her usual broad, smug grin, but it was still a false, constructed smile. An expression that concealed her true feelings, to an unnatural degree.

"That's so...sad," she said.

That moment, a shrill chiming rang from Yano-san's pocket.

When we parted at the gates, the words, "See you tomorrow," passed from neither of our lips.

As soon as I was alone, I began to run, recklessly. There was no need to, but I could not sit still, and so I ran. Before I knew it, I ended up high in the murky mountains. I slipped through the trees, passing by wild animals, and came out on the bank of a river. The rain poured down on my body, all the thoughts gone from my head.

In this form, I never grew cold. I was not cold, but I felt myself shivering, deep down inside. I closed my eyes and took a deep breath, but the trembling would not go away.

Sad. Sad. That's so...sad.

I couldn't get her smiling face out of my head.

I had accomplished what I set out to do that night. I had apologized. And I believed that she forgave me. That should have been a good thing.

And yet, I was shivering.

Yano-san had said it was sad that I was afraid of her.

The bullying, the fact that things had become so bad for her, that I had stepped on her precious birthday present, those things were not sad.

She said that it was sad that I was afraid.

I wasn't so stupid as to have no idea what she meant, once I thought about it. If someone was afraid of me, wouldn't I be sad? If someone wanted me to stay away from them, wouldn't I be sad? It wasn't so hard to imagine.

Especially if it was someone that I believed in.

Someone who, even if it wasn't the whole of them, there was at least some part I could believe in.

I'm sure that Yano-san probably believed in me.

No, not in my normal self. She believed in the me who would come all the way to the school at night to apologize, even after having done such a terrible thing.

So she had asked which was the real me—my day self, or my nighttime self. Surely, she hoped that my night self was my true self, which meant that the one who apologized to her was the real one, and the one who had done that awful deed was a fake.

But that wasn't the truth.

I didn't feel an ounce of guilt.

As I walked along the riverside, I saw two creatures before me: one great, one small. Thinking that I might be witnessing a hunt, I let out a roar, and both animals fled in separate directions.

And then I thought of Yano-san, who had stood her ground both before a larger classmate and before a monster.

Just what exactly had I hoped to accomplish in apologizing?

Did I intend to apologize and then do the same thing tomorrow if something else of hers landed in front of my feet again? Did I hope to say sorry, even though I would ignore her again tomorrow?

I was trying to create some point of compromise, all on my own.

I had hoped to apologize for my sake alone, so that I could pretend to be a kind person. So that I could pretend to be a model student.

"...I'm sorry."

I don't know who I was apologizing to, all alone there in that darkness. All I knew was that I was a far more hideous creature than the people who bullied Yano-san outright. The beast that hunted those weaker than itself in order to extend its own life was the most honest. The people who attacked those that they did not like, who made their stances clear, were the most transparent.

I abruptly looked down at my six feet as they crept along the ground. The black droplets skittered around the dirt, like countless tiny insects bringing their bodies together to form a living being. The longer I looked at it, the more repulsive it was.

Which was it?

Yano-san had surely been waiting for me. For me to come and see her during midnight break. For me, who, even if only at night, was like a friend to her. For me, who saw something in her.

For me, the monster.

She had waited for me, in this terrifying form of mine.

She had been deceived. I was a horrible creature.

I climbed the mountain, my eight eyes reflecting the pure darkness, my four tails swaying behind me. My field of vision, wider than that of any other living thing, was already so immersed in my own thoughts that I could not see the animals that cut across my path, nor the great trees rooted in the rock, nor the little flowers blooming quietly on the mountaintop.

Which was it?

Was it my form at night—a form of gathered black drops, sprouting six legs and eight goggling eyes? Was it my form during the day, my human form, which took part in bullying just to fit in? Or was it the tainted thing that nested inside of me, that always had, which had grown so large now as to consume the me that Yano-san had believed in?

Which one was it?

What truly was a monster?

Tuesday
DAY

BEFORE I KNEW IT, morning came.

My head felt heavy. I had let myself get soaked for so long in that form I had probably caught a cold.

My body felt sluggish, and the thought that I should stay home from school today flickered through my hazy head—but it was only a flicker. I descended to the first floor and ate the breakfast that my mother had prepared. I had only one piece of toast this morning.

Though it only occurred to me partway through changing into my uniform, I decided not to bother taking my temperature. Seeing it in numbers was sure to be disheartening.

Feeling my body's weakness reinforced the conviction that I was in fact stuck with this body. It was the opposite feeling of when I was flying through the skies at night. With the atmosphere and the sounds around, I could make believe that I was an entirely different existence from myself. Of course, just because I could didn't mean that I should.

When I stepped outside, it was no longer raining. However, I decided to walk.

Step by step, I walked the exact same path that I had yesterday. It was the same path that I had walked and biked countless times, but for the briefest of moments, it felt different than how it usually did. It must've been because of this cold or whatever.

I walked along with my head lowered, gazing at the puddles, when I suddenly saw a small pair of sneakers ahead of me.

"Mornin'!"

Before I could lift my eyes, I heard a girl's voice. The word alone was enough for me to distinguish who it was, but I was still surprised.

"Oh, mornin'. Weird seein' you here, Kudou."

I meant on this route to school. There were three main routes along which students typically commuted to our school, but Kudou lived along the northern path.

After laughing in her cheerful voice, she said, "Well, y'know." Even wrapped up in whatever heaviness had overtaken me, I had to laugh at the half-hearted answer.

"Well, y'know, *what?*" I asked.

"I stayed over at my sister's house, and she was gonna drive me to school, but I figured people would make fun of me since I usually ride my bike in, so I had her drop me off."

"Huh."

I was surprised to hear that Kudou, who seemed to be relatively enmeshed with the more athletic groups, was afraid of a thing like that, but I didn't say so out loud.

"Your sis used to be strongest member ever of the kendo club back in the day, yeah?"

"Yeah! There's a *lot* of pressure on me."

Kudou stuck out her tongue. She was a strong one. She could always make complaints or talk about things she hated with a smile. "Keep it up," I said, offering my heartfelt encouragement to the girl who always brightened my day. She returned a firm nod and a smile that showed her crooked teeth.

As I watched her nod, I suddenly thought—this cold or whatever was definitely doing my head in.

Which one was it? I thought again.

"Say Acchi, that reminds me..."

"Hm?"

Which one was it?

Kudou, who always tried to enjoy life to the fullest, always cheerfully looked after her juniors.

"You seem like you've been pretty down lately. Everything okay?"

Kudou, who would suddenly throw a drink carton at the back of a classmate's head in the middle of a conversation without hesitation.

"Seriously? I'm totally fine."

Which one was the real Kudou?

"That's good then. Seriously though, if anything's bothering you, you can tell me. I sit right next to you, after all."

"I mean, it's really nothing," I said.

I couldn't tell her that I might be a monster.

"Really?"

"...Hmm, I have been wondering if I should start getting serious about test prep."

"Whoa!"

I spun around, my hand to my head, as Kudou stopped walking and raised her voice in surprise.

"What?" I asked.

"No, I mean, it's just, I knew you were a serious guy, but wow."

Serious, she said. I put up my guard, thinking that I was being ridiculed...but I was wrong.

"I really need to start thinking about that, too. I'm not good enough at kendo to get into high school on just that. I need to follow your lead, Acchi. In exchange, I'll give you some of my chill!"

"Yeah, no thanks."

"Ahaha!"

She raised her voice in laughter. Honestly, that carefree nature of hers had saved me time and time again, and now, I felt that it might perhaps help me out again. I thought that, maybe I could ask Kudou—who never made fun of me for being serious, never made fun of people for being different from her. Even if the question itself was most certainly a strange one.

Still, I believed in Kudou.

"Now that you mention it, something else is kinda bothering me," I said in a breath.

Kudou quickly molded her face into a more serious expression.

"Oh, sure. Let's hear it."

"So, when you're with your teammates in the kendo club, and with the people in our class, and...you have a boyfriend now, don't you?"

"N-no, no way," she stammered.

"Well then, I guess when you were with your boyfriend before. Which of those times did you feel like the real you?"

"Uh, erm, well, I uh..." She hopped over a puddle. I walked around it. "I guess when I'm with you...and the others. When I'm with my club, I have to act properly as a third year, and when I was dating an older guy I was always on my toes."

"I see. Sorry for asking something so weird."

"Nah, it's fine."

She really didn't seem to mind the question; I was relieved. And then I began to fret, hearing that she knew exactly which one was her true self. Was everyone else like that, too? Was I the only one who didn't know?

Also, if that was true, then I wanted to know how bullying Yano-san fit in with that, but I was not about to push that far.

Until we arrived at school, I talked with Kudou about frivolous things, as always. It was a time when I didn't have to think about our class's shunning, or bullying, or revenge, or anything.

I thought the whole time about what Kudou had said, but I found no answer.

As we approached the school gates, there were suddenly more people around, and I saw Kasai in the midst of it, mouth open wide in a yawn. He noticed us as well and waved. Kudou and I waved back.

Then, Kudou suddenly sighed.

"I really am useless."

"At what?"

"Oh, uh, nothing."

She blushed uncharacteristically and covered her mouth as though she had spoken unconsciously or something. Despite my curiosity, I wasn't about to follow up. I didn't think she was useless, after all.

Kasai waited for us in front of the gates.

"Mornin'! You two always walk to school together?"

"Morning! I had my big sis drop me off nearby, and I met up with Acchi along the way."

Perhaps unable to stand how bored Kasai seemed as he grinned and gave empty responses, Kudou quickly changed the subject.

"It's nice that the rain stopped," she said.

We all crossed the school gates at our various paces, smiling at Kudou's appropriately put words.

Thus began another perfectly normal day of junior high school life.

I turned Kudou's words over again and again in my head.

The one who was truly useless was me, I thought.

Kudou lived her life every day, knowing exactly who she was, but I was different. Today I had come here yet again, knowing nothing at all, even though I was consumed with questions both night and day.

Surely, I should have decided by now.

Decided what, I don't know. But I felt that I should have decided *something* before coming here today.

And yet, here I was, beginning my day in the same way that I always did—still unable to even clearly say who I was and where I stood amongst our class.

At the shoe boxes, I changed into my indoor shoes—shoes that weren't soaked, weren't vandalized—and headed up the stairs alongside my classmates, who, unlike me, were not so cowardly.

I walked down the hallway, entered the classroom, and took my seat. Just as I had hundreds of times before. In the classroom, there were people who called out to me with a smile, people who were caught up in chattering about last night's TV programs, and people who were asleep facedown on their desks.

There was a monster sitting right here.

A liar, sitting right here.

And not one of them realized it.

None of them could tell my true form at a glance. Even I did not know what that was, after all. I still had yet to decide.

"Good...morning."

I still hadn't decided anything. Yet, there was that familiar odd voice.

I lifted my head, and as always, looked at her out of the cor-ner of my eye. Yano had entered the classroom through the front door, a self-satisfied grin on her face. Naturally, no one replied. A chill filled the room.

If only I could bring myself not to care about her, I thought. But trying not to care about her might mean exactly the same as caring about her.

Always.

As she greeted the classmates who she knew would just ignore her, Yano, as always, grinned smugly. I was the only one who knew there was more to it, that she wasn't just messed up.

I was the only one who knew that she did it because she was afraid.

Every morning, she smiled because she was afraid of something. Despite all that she had done.

Wasn't all this because she purposely made everyone so aware of her? Wasn't it because she took the time to speak to the people who bullied her? Wasn't it because of all her peculiar quirks and deeds? This was purely hypothetical, but all she had to do to alleviate the situation was to stop acting this way.

In other words, perhaps all of the day-to-day bullying was not the biggest source of her fear.

Perhaps it was even simpler than that. The answer wasn't that it was because she was the class whipping girl or because she was her own strange self.

It was a fear so simple that anyone could grasp it.

Perhaps what she feared most was that she would be ignored again today.

I saw each of Yano's steps as if in slow motion, as if sped up.

Of course, truthfully, it was neither. She walked as she always did, her limbs swaying, with our classmates occasionally recoiling in fear of rubbing sleeves with her.

All of my thoughts and emotions that had floated up throughout the night began to swirl within my mind.

I should have decided something before I met her again today.

I should have chosen something before I arrived.

Such as, who I was.

Such as, what a monster was.

Such as, what attitude I ought to take towards Yano.

Such as, what my true place was within this class.

If I hadn't decided, then all I had done last night had been for the sake of no one. I wouldn't have such worries if I just came to a decision, I thought.

And yet, I had thought the whole night through, and chosen nothing, decided nothing.

There was also the choice to think nothing at all. But I hadn't even decided whether I should do that.

I really, truly, had not decided anything at all. And yet...

"Good...morning."

The voice wove itself through the cracks between everyone in the room, resounding. It was a strange greeting, the voice wavering, the tone peculiar.

We were sensitive to these things. Our eyes and ears were sharper than the adults even realized, so that we could always spot things weaker than us, bad things. It never took us long to spot the odd one out.

I'm sure that everyone in the room heard that strange greeting. The flow of time soon returned to normal in the classroom, perhaps because it was typical if it was Yano who was that odd man out.

I don't think anyone actually realized who had spoken, nor who the words had been directed to.

Even I didn't know.

I have no idea why I would do such a thing, since I hadn't decided anything.

Only Yano, who was always grinning, looked right at me with surprise on her face.

She looked straight at me; the human, the monster.

She saw Acchi.

I swallowed thickly.

She was the only one who knew both of them.

She was the only one who knew both of my horrible forms.

And yet she did not avert her eyes one bit.

She regarded me wholly, as Acchi, with those two great big eyes.

She saw both sides of me.

The moment I realized that, I moved my mouth once more.

"Good morning."

The second time this greeting was spoken, everyone, including me, realized just who had said it and who the words were directed towards.

Yano knew as well. The greeting had reached her. I knew that it had from her lazy smile.

It wasn't her normal grin. The corners of her mouth were raised only slightly—a natural, unforced smile. Perhaps I was the only one who realized: this was her true smile.

"You finally found your...way," she said, her voice excessively loud. I didn't reproach her for it.

I thought about what I was doing.

Was I a traitor to our shared unity? Had I defected to Yano's side? I sifted through a lot of possible conclusions, but I really did not think it was all that serious. *Finally*, Yano had said, but I think even that was overstating it.

It was just a greeting. Nothing more than a simple greeting. That was something that either version of me could accomplish.

And yet...

"What gives?" asked Yano, tilting her short neck.

I thought she was asking me why I had decided to return her greeting today. Still, a greeting wasn't something that should arouse any suspicion.

I tried to answer, to convey that to her, my lips quivering so violently that even I could feel it, but that was wrong.

"Acchi-kun, why...are you crying?"

It was only when she said it that I noticed. My vision had gone hazy, and my throat felt tight. Something was running down my cheeks.

What was this? I didn't understand. Why should I be crying? I wasn't sad or anything.

Quickly, I wiped my face on my sleeve.

"Acchi, what's going on?" I heard Kudou ask from the seat beside me.

Somehow, I doubted that her concern was directed towards my tears.

She probably believed that I had gone off course. If that was what she thought, though, then I'm sorry to say it, but she was wrong.

The part of me that believed that Yano was strange was still there. The way she had treated Midorikawa, what she had done to Iguchi, that behavior was still twisted, still wrong. I could not abandon the part of me who believed that.

But I had finally come to realize that another *me* had been here all along as well. The *me* who thought that Yano might not be an entirely bad person. The *me* who couldn't believe that it was all right to bully a girl who loved talking about the music, manga, and movies she enjoyed. That *me* had been here all along, and not only at night.

I hadn't decided anything.

Even after thinking the whole night through, I was unable to choose a single course.

But I knew now, I realized, that both of my selves were reflected in Yano's eyes.

The me of the night, who could not ignore Yano-san.

The *me* of the day, who did not want to be hated.

Neither of them was a good person.

And so neither me could save you.

But I could at least hear your voice and return it in kind.

That was something that either side of me could do.

Perhaps it was strange, perhaps it was incomprehensible.

Perhaps it was even a little messed up.

But if just talking to someone was messed up, then I'd lost my way a while ago.

I'd been living my life without knowing which direction each side of me would lean, and when. I had reached the limit of what I could do while living in that indecision.

Ah—I could see now. I was always one step behind Yano in figuring these things out.

Now I knew the reason for my tears.

I had finally found my way.

And so I told Kudou, "Nothing's going on."

That reply might have sounded to Kudou like a definitive declaration, a statement that I was allying myself with Yano. But it wasn't. I was the same as I ever was. Last night, there had been something worrying me. This morning I had run into Kudou, talked about it, and cheered up a bit. This was perfectly in line with the normal everyday existence that I always lived.

Of course, I knew that my classmates would not accept someone as indecisive as me so simply. I couldn't forget what had happened to Iguchi, once her half-hearted stance was revealed.

And yet, I had hope.

Hope that one day, they all might realize it, too.

It wasn't a leap to imagine that they could be in the same spot. They might be right there, within the pain of others. They might be mistaken in believing that they knew exactly who they were.

We might *all* be messed up, each in our own different ways. We might not all have a defined place.

I had come to realize this.

And so, I knew that Kudou was different from me, as she responded in her own messed-up way, scooting her desk away from mine and glaring at me.

Her eyes looked like Nakagawa's had when looking at Iguchi.

It was difficult to accept that.

I felt sadness, from the bottom of my heart.

When you're suddenly in that person's shoes, you can no longer believe "That's just the way things are."

Realizing this for the first time shocked me all over again.

That night,
*   I slept soundly, for the first time in a while.*